THE
FINAL
CUT

THE
FINAL
CUT

A NOVEL BY

Robert Westbrook

BASED ON THE MOTION PICTURE
WRITTEN AND DIRECTED BY

Omar Naïm

AN ONYX BOOK

ONYX
Published by New American Library, a division of
Penguin Group (USA) Inc., 375 Hudson Street,
New York, New York 10014, U.S.A.
Penguin Books Ltd, 80 Strand,
London WC2R 0RL, England
Penguin Books Australia Ltd, 250 Camberwell Road,
Camberwell, Victoria 3124, Australia
Penguin Books Canada Ltd, 10 Alcorn Avenue,
Toronto, Ontario, Canada M4V 3B2
Penguin Books (NZ), cnr Airborne and Rosedale Roads,
Albany, Auckland 1310, New Zealand

Penguin Books Ltd, Registered Offices:
80 Strand, London WC2R 0RL, England

First published by Onyx, an imprint of New American Library,
a division of Penguin Group (USA) Inc.

First Printing, August 2004
10 9 8 7 6 5 4 3 2 1

PUBLISHER'S NOTE
This is a work of fiction. Names, characters, places, and incidents either
are the product of the author's imagination or are used fictitiously, and
any resemblance to actual persons, living or dead, business establishments,
events, or locales is entirely coincidental.

THE CUTTERS' CODE

1. IT IS FORBIDDEN FOR A CUTTER TO HAVE A ZOE IMPLANT.

2. IT IS FORBIDDEN FOR A CUTTER TO SELL OR GIVE AWAY ZOE FOOTAGE TO OUTSIDE PARTIES.

3. IT IS FORBIDDEN TO MIX FOOTAGE FROM TWO DIFFERENT ZOE IMPLANTS OR TO CREATE NEW FOOTAGE WITH THE AID OF COMPUTERS.

ONE

In the beginning there is light. At first, only a tiny shaft is shining from the far end of a long tunnel; then slowly it grows brighter and brighter.

But soon the light is too intense, unbearable to bear. We would look away if we could. We would return inside, where it is warm and dark and safe, but we can't. Already it's too late. We are caught in the surge and the squeeze; a river of motion carries us forward through the ooze of mucus and blood.

Out we go, on and on . . . until there we are, like it or not, hanging by the feet from a hand gloved in latex, and all around us a strange white world we did not ask for. Everything is a little blurry. People speak and their voices echo in our ears, creating confusion we cannot understand.

Then a woman on a bed reaches for us and there is love in her eyes. A cord connects us to the woman, and there is blood and water everywhere. A man takes hold of us and cuts the umbilical cord. Snap! It's gruesome beyond belief to experience all this, but fortunately the man wraps us in a clean white cloth and hands us to the woman on the bed.

With a great howl, a scream of life, we're beginning to get a grip on the situation. We are a baby boy, and we have just been born.

TWO

The room inside the Cleopatra Hotel was sterile as a hospital: cold and modern, not an object out of place. Alan Hakman sat in front of the monitor watching the birth, the blue light of the screen flickering on his face. He was a man with haunted eyes, no longer young but not yet old: a man caught in the indecisive midst of drab middle age, not someone you would notice on the street. He wore glasses, his face was cold and pale, revealing nothing. His eyes were wary and watchful. Outside in the city, night had fallen many hours ago, but Alan's concentration remained focused on the screen, as he blocked out all other thoughts and ignored the man hovering near his shoulder.

Near Alan's hand, there was a notebook with an ivory talisman on a leather hoop tucked inside as a bookmark. The talisman was unexpected, not the usual sort of personal frill for a man like Alan. Occasionally, barely taking his eyes from the monitor, he scribbled hurried notes, ideas of sequence and timing, how he might recut this unfinished footage into a work of art and also satisfy the family's expectations—he must never forget that.

On the screen, life itself continued. It was remarkable to be in a hospital delivery room, watching a birth from the baby's point of view. In the lower right hand corner of the screen there was a name and age display. It read simply:

D. MONROE: 0 YEARS: 0 DAYS: 21 HOURS

The baby shivered and cried as he looked about in astonishment, his first very limited view of planet Earth. All around him, people were talking and laughing.

Now, slowly, classical music swelled in the background, a soundtrack that gradually became more insistent, expressing the beauty of the moment. This was where the artistry came in, of course, creating emphasis, making a moment more important.

There was a dissolve and the scene changed from the hospital to a summer day on a suburban lawn. In the lower right-hand corner the display now read:

D. MONROE: 3 YEARS: 98 DAYS: 13 HOURS

The scene on the monitor remained from the child's point of view, from the eyes of a three-year-old scanning the miracle of existence. The screen showed the small hands of Danny Monroe as they rested on the handlebars of a red tricycle. In one of Danny's hands, there was a third of a jam sandwich, and on the ground beyond the handlebars, dozens of tiny black ants swarmed over an anthill, carrying away sandwich crumbs on their backs as they scuttled up the anthill and down into their hole.

What was fascinating about the scene was its utter authenticity. It existed entirely from the child's viewpoint as he experienced the moment, as though he had a camera in his brain. The eyes scanned away from the anthill toward Danny's mother, who was nearby watering the lawn with a hose. This was Eliza Monroe. She was in her early thirties, a pretty woman in a large straw hat and a bright yellow bathing suit.

She turned toward the monitor and spoke. "Danny, come here, sweetie. Get away from those ants!" Her voice sounded distant and hollow, like an audio recording that had degraded over time. This was unfortunate, a small technical problem that Alan would need to fix. Meanwhile, on the monitor, Danny looked down at the ants one last time; then he began to pedal toward his mother, his small hands and the handlebars moving bumpily over the lawn.

There was another gush of classical music as the scene changed from the summer lawn to the interior of the Monroe station wagon, still from Danny's point of view. It was daytime and the car was traveling. Outside the windows, trees and blue sky rushed past. The display read:

D. MONROE: 7 YEARS: 127 DAYS: 8 HOURS

Danny was in the backseat with his younger brother, Jason, and they were playing with

6

plastic action figures. In the front seat, there were Mr. Monroe and Mrs. Monroe—parents, large figures of authority who sometimes turned around and told Danny and his brother to behave. Even without the display, it was obvious from Danny's voice and height that he was now several years older.

"My guy steals your guy's gun and blasts him," Danny said to his brother. The sound quality was better in this sequence, more natural.

"Can't!" Jason answered. "It's attached to my leg!"

Meanwhile, in the hotel room, Alan, curious to see the other man's reaction, glanced up briefly from the monitor. The man was Jason Monroe, the young kid from long ago. But he was now in his sixties, thin and stooped with leathery skin and long gray hair. He bore little resemblance to the child on the monitor.

"Oh, my God! That's me, man!" Jason cried. His eyes filled with emotion to see himself—actually *see* himself—through the eyes of his older brother.

Alan smiled thinly. The emotional impact on relatives and friends as they relived the moments of their lives was always the same. On the monitor, the scene had now switched from the station wagon to a bedroom at night. At the lower right-hand corner of the screen, the display read:

D. MONROE: 27 YEARS: 11 DAYS:
20 HOURS

Years had passed and now Danny Monroe was a father, his hand reaching into the frame to hold the tiny finger of a baby boy as the infant rocked back and forth in a cradle.

"Hey, what's that music you're using?" Jason asked. "I really dig it."

Alan remained silent, his face an impenetrable mask. He preferred not to talk about the details of his work to customers; it was better they simply experience the magic.

"Whatever it is, it's terrific, man," Jason said. "It really . . . I dunno . . . suits his life somehow."

And of course, that was it exactly: the art of being a cutter, finding the right music, the right tempo . . . and knowing what to leave out, of course. Discretion was an important part of Alan's job. Frankly, there were moments of customers' lives—weeks, months, sometimes entire years—that were important to leave out. For everyone's sake. Jason turned his head back to the monitor. The two men were watching Jason's brother's life on Alan's Chop Block, a special laptop computer that was dull gray and metallic with a screen seventeen inches wide.

Now the scene changed again, to Danny celebrating a birthday party with a group of close friends. It was apparent that Danny was a little drunk.

"Thank you. Thanks to all of you," Danny was saying enthusiastically, slurring his words. "Best birthday ever!"

Alan touched a button and the image on the screen froze. He stood up and switched on a lamp.

"That's some of the opening sequence," he said to Jason. "The rest needs a few fixes and tweaks, but he's clocking in at an hour and forty minutes."

"Yeah, that's cool. I just wanted to have a look before the Rememory tomorrow. To make sure it was what we wanted. You know?" Jason laughed nervously, leaving many things unsaid. "But you've done a hell of a job with him, Mr. Hakman. You've done the son of a bitch right."

Jason lowered his head and hesitated. Clearly, he wanted to ask a favor, though he wasn't certain he had the right. Alan waited silently, accustomed to these awkward moments with clients. It was part of being a cutter: the human angle, dealing with people who had just lost someone they loved . . . or perhaps secretly hated.

"I don't suppose . . . There was a fishing trip when we were thirteen," Jason said. "Just Danny and I and Dad."

"At the Cape," Alan said.

"Yes, yes. That one! My God, that day is still with me. Is it . . . ?"

"You requested it specifically," Alan reminded him. "It's there."

Jason smiled happily. "Well, I'll be off then."

Alan accompanied his client to the door. In the hallway, Jason shook his head in amazement, then walked away. When he was alone, Alan closed the door and returned to his laptop. The image of the birthday party was still frozen on the screen. Alan sat down in front of the console and brought up a menu on the screen with the tap of a button.

The computer announced itself with an electronic voice, female and bland: *"Closing Zoe Project D. Monroe. Rough cut six."*

Alan hit a few more buttons.

"Opening D. Monroe scene 127-Q," said the computer.

Instantly, the screen filled with a new image from Danny's point of view, but this one was not nearly as pleasant as those that came before. A half-naked woman was on the ground, crouching in fear. She was battered and bruised and bleeding at the side of her mouth. At the bottom of the screen, the display marked the precise moment of Danny's life when this violence occurred:

D. MONROE: 35 YEARS: 255 DAYS:
22 HOURS

"Oh, God . . . oh, please . . . oh, please don't . . . don't," the woman screamed.

Alan listened to her agonized shriek. There was always something shabby about violence in real life, not at all the thrilling stuff of cinema. A sickening crunch sounded as Danny hit the woman again and again, letting loose his remorseless anger. Watching the horror on the monitor in front of him, Alan showed no emotion. He had watched such scenes before in his profession: the less savory moments of a lifetime. As far as Alan was concerned, he might as well have been staring at a wall.

On the screen, the woman kept screaming. Then, in the background, there was a scrape of metal against concrete. Danny was lifting some weapon not visible to the monitor.

"Oh, please, Danny, oh, please!" the woman begged. "Danny, you motherfucker . . . oh, fucking Jesus Gooooddddddd . . ."

Alan hit the DELETE button and the horror ended instantly, bringing silence to the hotel room.

"*Scene 127-Q . . . deleted,*" the computer said, confirming his action.

Alan stretched his neck with an audible snap, the only sign of tension in his body. He poked several buttons, and the screen went dark. It took him a few moments to close up his Chop Block editing console and lock the machine so that no one could use it in his absence. At last, he stood and left the hotel room, shutting the door behind him, putting the revised and edited life of D. Monroe out of mind.

Outside, the night was dark and anonymous. Alan made his way along a narrow downtown street to the subway, passing through a crowd of strangers. On city streets, people averted their eyes, keeping their private thoughts and concerns to themselves. But Alan knew them, their thoughts, and their concerns, or he could imagine them well enough.

Editing other people's lives made Alan feel a little like God. Alan relished the idea. With quick steps, he descended into the subway.

THREE

At the age of fifty-one, Alan Hakman himself had memories he often wished he could delete. Sometimes it seemed as though it would be much better to recall other people's memories rather than his own, but doing so wasn't entirely possible, of course—not even for a cutter.

There was one central moment of Alan's childhood that wouldn't leave him alone. It returned relentlessly, and always when he least expected—such as the very moment when he was riding uptown in the subway.

Blue sky, a bored afternoon, a construction site, the sun pouring down. Time seemed to stand still on such an afternoon, nothing moving.

The memory always brought a queasy feeling in his stomach, a lingering guilt that wouldn't leave him alone. He could see the scene so clearly. He was a child sitting cross-legged in the dirt playing with marbles. It was the day he had met the kid with the thick glasses in the empty lot.

Alan remembered wearing a red shirt—how he remembered this particular detail after all these years, he couldn't say. The incident had started simply enough. Marbles! Sitting in the dirt, Alan took careful aim and let one of the marbles fly . . . only to miss by a foot. He sat watching as the marble rolled up against someone's shoe. That was when Alan looked up to see a boy about his own age. The other child was wearing amazingly thick glasses and peering down at Alan.

"Can I play?" the boy with glasses asked.

"Do you have any marbles?"

"Yeah." Without waiting for a further invitation, the bespectacled boy crouched down and set his handful of marbles in the dirt. He was probably lonely too that afternoon. Lonely and bored. The boy took off his glasses to clean them roughly on his shirt. Then he propped them back on his nose and took aim with his marble. *Crack!* A direct hit.

"Good shot!" Alan cried, greatly impressed.

They had become friends immediately in the sudden way such alliances happen in childhood. Funny how Alan could see his past all so clearly, every detail as if it was yesterday, though in fact the meeting had happened more than forty years ago. He could close his eyes and smell the dust of that empty lot. Absurd, really, an insignificant game of marbles, how could something so small have cast such a long shadow on a life . . . ?

A loud rumble brought Alan back to the present, in the subway car, which was half-empty and imbued with a kind of loneliness that the trains always had late at night as they delivered tired people to their destinations. Alan's eyes focused on a large colorful advertisement on the opposite wall. The image, a product of cutting-edge technology, moved every few seconds, showing four smiling children at play on a beach. Beneath the moving picture there was a caption:

THE ZOE IMPLANT FROM EYE TECH—
EVERYTHING YOU EXPERIENCE

Alan smiled thinly. Near him on the bench, a man and a woman were also studying the poster. The woman was obviously pregnant, with only a few weeks to go before she would deliver.

"You think we'll be able to afford one?" she asked her husband.

The man rubbed her belly and smiled. Alan would have enjoyed to continue watching them, but his stop was coming up. He stood as the train rumbled into the station. After the doors hissed open, he stepped aside for a tattooed man, who was barreling into the car from the platform. The man's head was shaved and on his face and head he had tattooed the symbols for "REWIND," "PLAY," "FAST FORWARD," "PAUSE," and "STOP." Alan knew well enough what these tattoos meant, and he tried to make his exit without attracting attention. Unfortunately, the man bumped into him, stared down quickly at the Chop Block in Alan's hand, then looked up menacingly. Alan slipped onto the platform, relieved when the doors closed behind him. Life was not without danger in cities.

He made his way up from the subway platform to the street. Buildings loomed in the darkness, musty and grim. The neighborhood was old, falling into disrepair, dimly lit and quiet. Alan's steps echoed along the pavement as he approached the entrance to the October Theater, an aging movie palace with a darkened marquee. Inside the theater, the ornate lobby was nearly empty, save for a few tables and chairs surrounded by old movie posters from a long-ago era. Three people were seated around one of the tables, two men and a woman.

Hasan, a vivid, handsome man in his thirties, was in the middle of a story, speaking loudly. "This girl was a total fuckup. In and out of schools, drinking, drugs. Then she turns twenty-one and finds out about her Zoe Implant. Complete one eighty. She's born again. Her knowing that someone would one day *watch* . . . transforms her into this kind, gentle, loving person."

"So what happened?" asked the second man at the table. He was about twenty years old, wiry and pale, hardly more than a scrawny kid.

"Suicide," Hasan answered with a shrug. "Took a dive off of her balcony, twenty-seven floors straight onto her head." He banged the table for emphasis. "Her implant was vaporized. They fished around in her brain goop, but not a trace."

"Charming little story, Hasan," said Thelma, whom Alan had known for years. She was in her fifties, but still bristling with sexuality. She had an air of dignified flamboyance that commanded attention. "Do go on," she said, her tone edged with irony.

Just then Hasan noticed Alan. His eyes lit with joyful malice. "Now here's a rare treat," he said.

Silently, Alan joined the group at the table.

"Michael, this is Alan Hakman. Mikey is my new assistant," Thelma said, indicating the skinny kid.

Alan nodded a brief hello. It was hard to keep up with Thelma's assistants. She seemed to have a new one every week. "What happened to Eddie?" he asked.

"Ah, Eddie freaked out on me. Wasn't cut out for the business. Strung too tight."

Hasan handed Alan a bright red flyer. "Have you seen these things? They're all over town."

Alan examined the flyer without expression. In fact, he had seen the red flyers plastered to streetlights and the sides of buildings. The headline read:

ZOE IMPLANTS ARE UNHOLY

"Anti-Zoe hippies always sounded crazy to me . . . but now they sound *crazy*!" Hasan said. He snatched the flyer back from Alan's hand and read aloud, adding emphasis: " 'It is not our *place* to see through other people's *eyes*. That is for *God* and for God *alone*.' " He put down the flyer and made a whistling sound through his teeth to show his contempt. He turned his attention back to Alan. "So . . . how's the Monroe project going?"

"Fine," Alan told him.

"Just fine?"

"Just fine."

Hasan exchanged a conspiratorial glance with Thelma, who smirked knowingly. "I guess if you take the dirty projects you learn to keep your dirty mouth shut," he said amicably, giving Alan a slap on the back. Hasan turned to Michael. "It's your good luck to meet this guy. Best cutter in town.''

Michael made an effort to look impressed. ''Who's your assistant?'' he asked.

''I don't have an assistant.''

'' 'Cause I have a friend looking to get into the racket,'' Michael went on blindly, missing the edge in Alan's reply. ''She's real talented and eager and everything. Maybe you could meet with her—''

''I don't have an assistant,'' Alan said more forcefully, and though Michael appeared annoyed by the brush-off, Alan ignored him. ''You have anything for me, Thelma?''

''Straight to business.'' She flashed a nasty smile and took a moment to light a cigarette. ''I got a job last week that I passed on. I think it's right up your alley. You know Charles Bannister? His widow is looking for a cutter.''

''Bannister?'' Michael asked, interrupting. He seemed impressed. ''The Eye Tech lawyer?''

Thelma nodded, exhaling smoke like a dragon. ''Was out jogging when his heart collapsed.''

"Eye Tech let his footage out?" Hasan asked.

"Jennifer Bannister won a lawsuit against them and claimed her husband's implant. She insisted on hiring her own cutter. With good reason, too."

"We could've taken that job! After Caldwell, our schedule's wide-open!" Michael said, agitated at the thought of missing out on a big job. For a skinny kid, he was very pushy.

Alan made a point of studying his fingernails. Michael annoyed him on a visceral level. There were too many kids like this one coming into the field only for the money, with no love for the art of the profession.

Puffing on her cigarette, Thelma glanced shrewdly at the three men. A connoisseur of undertones, she saw very well how her assistant grated on Alan. "I don't like the ugly stuff. It gives me nightmares. And this pig Bannister, he's human garbage. I took one look at his footage and sent it right back." She turned to Alan. "Anyway, she only hired me because you were busy with Monroe. It's you she wants." Her eyes moved to Michael.

"Our friend Alan here, this is his specialty, so to speak. If you can't bear to look at it, he will."

Thelma scribbled an address and phone number on a napkin and slid the napkin over to Alan. "Drop by there tomorrow. I'll let her know. She'll be expecting you."

She glanced at her watch, stubbed out her cigarette, and stood to leave. Michael rose also, following her lead. "Rememory's in two days," she explained, "and we're still cutting picture. Goddamn last-minute jobs."

"They keep you young," Hasan said vaguely.

Thelma left with Michael in tow, disappearing into the street from the theater lobby. At the table, Alan carefully folded the napkin with Jennifer Bannister's address and put it in his pocket.

"Alan, you look so down all the time. Come have a few drinks with me," Hasan suggested. "I've been tinkering with a new sorting program for the Guillotine. Love to get your feedback on it."

The Guillotine, as it was called, was the master console of the cutting trade, where people's lives were edited. Discussing a new software program interested Alan more than a drink, but still he declined.

"Maybe another time," he answered, standing up to leave.

"Another time then," Hasan agreed, watching thoughtfully as Alan disappeared into the night.

FOUR

Alan didn't feel much like going home. He was in a restless mood, uninterested in facing the silence of his apartment. Ignoring the taxis that occasionally buzzed by, he walked across town until he came to a small bookstore on a quiet side street. A sign in the window announced the sale of used and rare books. Undecided, Alan peered inside the window for a long while. It seemed to him that such was his fate: always the watcher, the man on the outside.

At last, getting up his nerve, he entered the store. The bell over the door tinkled behind him. The interior of the bookstore was cozy, crowded, and pleasant. Shelves were stacked high with leather-bound volumes and yellowed paperbacks. One or two late-night browsers wandered the aisles, but otherwise business was slow. Alan made his way among the shelves until he saw Delila near the rear of the store. She was leafing through the pages of an old book, with a meditative look, both romantic and thoughtful, that suited her well. Alan silently enjoyed having a moment to behold her before she saw him. Delila—her name was wonderful . . . and a little dangerous. She was the owner of the bookstore: mid-thirties, dark hair, trim, lovely, her eyes full of beauty and life. The store's single employee, an elderly woman Alan didn't much like, stood near Delila. The older woman was musty and sour; she perpetually had a disapproving look on her face. Suddenly coming to a conclusion, Delila closed the book in her hand decisively and handed the volume to her employee.

"Please, this is a history book," she said. "It shouldn't be shelved with fiction."

Without a word, the other woman disappeared up the narrow stairs to the second floor. Delila turned toward Alan, fixing him with a hard, far-from-friendly stare. He realized she had been aware of him the entire time. Delila missed nothing; she had simply been deciding what attitude to take.

"What do you want?" she demanded.

"Delila, I just want to talk."

"I'm busy," she said. She rolled her eyes ironically. "Store's still open. It's the eleven thirty rush. Books are flying off the shelves."

Alan felt awkward. As an introverted person, he had trouble playing the relationship game. But he made an effort in the case of Delila.

"I . . . I missed you and I wanted to see you."

Her eyes, lovely and unimpressed, opened with incredulity.

"Really? That's nice. What's the matter with you? We've tried this over and over, Alan, and we're just no good together!"

"I know," he agreed. "But I'll cha—"

"But you can't," she said. "You're a man of marble. Forget it. Forget me." Delila began to walk down the aisle.

Alan trailed silently behind her, unwilling to let her go. "I still have some of your things," he said clumsily. "You want me to drop them off?"

"Keep them," she said without looking at him. "Souvenirs."

"You want to come pick them up?"

Delila stopped and faced him. Alan was not certain what she saw, but he had the sense that in his entire life, no one had ever *seen* him quite as fully as Delila did. She studied him as though he were an obscure book that had to be catalogued. It was as though her gaze illuminated every dark corner of his soul.

To his surprise, a smile, playing like sunlight on her lips, gradually came to her face. He wished he understood women better.

Was there a chance for him after all?

Alan turned the key in his lock, then opened the door to his apartment. Delila followed him inside.

"I see nothing has changed," she said, looking around.

Alan's apartment was one large room, a spacious studio. Like his work space at the Cleopatra Hotel, the apartment was clean and perfectly in order. A number of dim lamps illuminated the room, indirect lighting, very discreet. He watched Delila as she wandered through the studio. Dozens of mirrors lined the walls and stood on shelves and furniture.

She moved past carefully arranged shelves of books, CDs, and boxes of electronic gear. At one side of the room, Alan's bed had its sheets tucked in and its pillow smoothed. In the opposite corner was a small kitchenette so clean and proper it looked as though it had never been used.

Delila made her way toward the far end of the room, where her gaze fell on Alan's editing console. The machine resembled a large wooden desk with monitors on one side—wood and chrome, an aesthetic combination of old and new. The face of the console was dotted with buttons, levers, and dials. Printed on the face was the brand name: GUILLOTINE. An unfortunate name for cutting equipment, but descriptive. The Guillotine, surrounded by supplementary decks, devices, power sources, and extension cords, dominated the far end of Alan's apartment.

Delila touched the cool chrome surface of the Guillotine, letting her fingers run along the monitors.

"Guillotine," she said thoughtfully.

Alan had gathered the clothing she had left behind. He held several shirts and a shoebox, the remnants of their brief life together.

With her hand idly caressing the monitors, Delila allowed her gaze to move from Alan to her belongings, then back to Alan again. She seemed to be having trouble imagining that she had ever lived here. "You're like a mortician," she told him, "or a priest . . . or a taxidermist—all of them."

"Please, don't . . . don't touch the Guillotine." The words simply escaped his lips. He knew it was the wrong thing to say, but he couldn't help himself.

She sighed. But her hand rose from the monitor. "And you wonder why it didn't work," she said. "The biggest part of yourself is off-limits to everyone."

Decisively, Delila grabbed the shirts and the shoe box from Alan and began to leave. Alan struggled with himself, trying to think of a way to keep her.

"Is that what it is?" he asked. "You want to see . . . *them*?"

Delila stopped in her tracks and turned. "I mean, you get to see life upon life," she told him. "Most of us get only one—if that! What are people's lives like? Do they make any sense? It seems so massive and so random."

"You've never been to a Rememory?"

She shook her head. "No. Well, once . . . a few years ago, for an old boyfriend of mine. Before you and I met. But I couldn't take it. I didn't stay."

Alan gave her a curious look. "Why not?"

"Because the film wasn't . . . it wasn't him. I prefer to remember my own way."

Alan walked over to the editing console and opened a drawer. He selected a set of disks that sat apart from the others. From his jacket pocket, he brought out a pair of glasses and put them on so he could see the small writing better. He flipped through the disk, picked one out, and inserted it into the Guillotine. He touched a red switch and the largest of the monitors popped to life.

Delila was watching him carefully, still holding her belongings, looking like she might bolt at any moment. He motioned for her to sit in his editing chair. She hesitated briefly, but her curiosity got the better of her. She sat down.

Alan peered over her shoulder as the monitor hissed with static, showing at first only a screen of black. Then the Zoe film began, a montage that Alan had put together, all of the same person gazing into a mirror at different stages of his life.

The first shot was of a young boy, about seven years old, staring into the bathroom mirror with sleepy eyes. He was in his pajamas. He looked as though it were the end of a long day and he could hardly stay awake another moment more. Drowsily, he reached for his toothbrush.

The scene dissolved and now, a few years older, he was shaving for the first time. The teenage boy stared intently at the mirror, then winced as he cut himself. He looked down at the sink, where a few droplets of blood mixed with the water and shaving foam.

Now he was in his early twenties, a young man with a scruffy beard. The mirror was cracked and dirty and clearly the circumstances of his life had changed. As he gazed into the mirror, a young woman came up beside him and kissed him on the cheek. He smiled at her reflection.

Another dissolve and he was older, popping in contact lenses.

Now he was in his late twenties, emerging

from the shower, grabbing hold of a towel to wipe himself dry.

The time sped forward maniacally, a lifetime in progress, severely edited. Every passing moment, however, was set in a bathroom, giving the film a weird thematic unity. Soon the man in the Zoe film was in his thirties, gingerly inspecting a black eye. Then he was in his forties, carefully trimming his graying mustache with a pair of scissors, his eyes held steady as he moved his face from side to side.

At last, the man was in his sixties, his hair gray, his eyes sunken. He reached for his toothbrush and began to clean his teeth with solemn determination. Then suddenly he paused and grimaced in pain. Holding his chest, he coughed violently into the sink. He wiped his mouth with the back of his hand and saw blood. He was breathing hard, gasping for breath, frightened. The point of view seemed to go crazy until the angle of the scene lurched downward into the sink. Now there was more blood swirling down the drain . . . like a life dripping away.

Slowly, the scene became brighter and brighter, fading to white. The meaning was all too obvious. There would be no more mirrors for this particular Zoe subject. Unable to speak at first, Delila stared into the blank monitor.

"How awful," she said finally. "What about all the bits in between?"

"It's not awful," Alan told her. "It's . . . symmetrical. Geometric. Beautiful."

She turned from the screen to face him. "Beautiful? How is it beautiful? He just . . . gets older and older, then dies. There's no life there. Just clean teeth."

Delila giggled at her joke, but stopped when she saw that Alan was not laughing. His profession—his art—was a very serious matter.

"It's better this way, without the clutter," he assured her in a tone that left no room for discussion.

She leaned closer as a silence settled between them. He beheld her face only inches from his own and tried to understand her.

"I did miss you," she said. "My enigmatic riddle . . ."

As always, she made the first move, kissing his neck. Alan's awkwardness slowly melted as they began to kiss and caress each other. Her lips were familiar, yet an utter mystery.

Her tongue explored his mouth. She tasted wonderful and enticing. There was a softness to her, a graceful glide of her body against him. His hand seemed to move on its own volition from her slim waist up to her breast.

Things got hot quickly, the old lust rushing back. After a few moments, she led him from the editing console toward the bed, both of them shedding clothes on the floor, stepping out of shirts, trousers, skirt, and underwear in an impatient frenzy. They fell onto the bed almost crazy for each other. She was the more aggressive, kissing, biting, pressing against him. Naked, skin against skin. It was magic, beyond words, urgent. He was about to enter her, and she was ready. But then, all at once, she noticed that Alan's eyes were not on her. He was going through the physical motions of lovemaking, but his attention was somewhere else.

Delila turned and saw what had distracted him. Alan was watching their reflection in one of his mirrors. A surge of furious anger flooded through her. She leaped up from the bed and stepped away.

"For God's sake, Alan! I'm right here in front of you!"

Violently, she flipped the mirror with her

37

hand so that it faced the wall. Meanwhile, Alan sat up on the bed with a shamed expression. Delila stormed about the apartment and collected her belongings. He had never seen her move so quickly, as though she couldn't bear his presence another second more. In a flash, she was at the door, half dressed and on her way out of his life.

"I see *nothing* has changed!" she cried. Then she slammed the door behind her.

Alan sat on his bed and felt the enormous emptiness of Delila's absence. A dreadful silence settled upon his apartment, which was again empty of the life she always brought with her. He knew he was to blame, yet it was beyond him to figure out exactly what he had done. The whole matter was an emotional blur he could not penetrate. After several minutes, he stood and walked over to the mirror Delila had disturbed. He turned it around so he could see his own image, his eyes peering back at him.

He wondered who the lonely stranger staring back at him with haunted eyes was? Alan really couldn't say. The mirror was precise, an honest broker, yet it told him nothing of the mysteries inside.

FIVE

For Alan, memories were also a way of looking in a mirror; but it was a jagged mirror of broken glass, one that cast imperfect reflections. Like shards, these memories drew blood.

The afternoon at the empty lot was now forty-two years in the past, yet it remained with Alan constantly, a present fact. He and the boy with the thick glasses had played marbles until they got bored. After a while, they counted their marbles and divided the stash; then they began walking together in no particular direction, just killing time.

"What's your name?" Alan had asked.

"Louis. Yours?"

"Alan."

He was nine and Louis about the same age. In Alan's memory, the afternoon seemed larger and brighter than any afternoon had been ever since. The boys walked through an oddly desolate landscape on the edge of a city of deserted streets, a place of open fields and low buildings.

"You're not from here, are you?" Louis had asked.

"No," Alan answered. "I'm here with my parents for the day. They have some stuff they need to do."

The boys approached a construction site. There was an unfinished building, a concrete shell several stories high that was empty and abandoned. It was just a dusty place where adults worked, and yet it exerted a strong fascination. There were unfamiliar objects lying in piles: twisted lengths of metal rebar, odd assortments of lumber and brick. The windows had not yet been fitted with glass; they were only empty holes gazing down upon the street like watchful eyes.

"What is in there?" Alan asked.

He ran off toward the unfinished building with Louis following reluctantly behind. Alan climbed inside the facade past a clutter of construction debris. The interior was eerie, with stairs that wound up dangerously to unfinished floors and balconies. Alan liked the strangeness of being there, the sense of forbidden adventure. He picked up a metal pipe and began to etch his name on one of the concrete walls. It was satisfying to leave his mark behind. He was about to write his last name when Louis came up next to him.

"Don't do that! We aren't even allowed to be here," Louis cautioned.

But Alan was having fun; his parents were not around and he was in no mood to be cautious. He admired his handiwork for a moment, then pointed to the unfinished staircase.

"What's up there?" Without waiting for an answer, he ran up the steps, two at a time, even though there was no railing, nothing but gaping space to the hard clutter below.

"No! Alan, you're going to get me in trouble," Louis called. When Alan didn't answer, Louis chased after him up the stairs. It wasn't too scary, as long as you didn't look down.

Up they went, Alan in the lead and Louis following, high into the airy skeleton of the building. There was a second floor, a third, and still the stairs kept climbing into the unfinished heights. Alan was a little frightened now, though of course he wouldn't say so. Danger was what made it all such an adventure. Danger and no grown-ups anywhere around to tell them what to do.

At nine years old, he had believed himself immortal. He hadn't learned yet about the fragility of experience. . . .

But now someone was speaking, a woman, causing the memory to vanish from Alan's mind: *I can see the grass. I can hear it crunching beneath our feet.*

Reluctantly, Alan returned to the present. He was standing on the driveway outside a sprawling house on a large piece of land. There were shade trees and a gently rolling lawn, with every blade of grass cut just right. The flower beds, a tad too perfect for a private home, were obviously tended with military precision by professional gardeners. This was the Bannister mansion, owned by the widow of the Eye Tech lawyer who had died jogging. Alan had come to see the widow about a possible job, and she was going on and on about a distant memory. Of course, that was part of being a cutter; people treated you as though you were a cross between a priest and a psychologist, telling you all their secrets.

"The house was big. Enormous," Jennifer Bannister was saying, describing the incident from her past. "Like this one. We didn't care whose house it was."

They walked inside as Mrs. Bannister continued her story. Alan had a glimpse of a young girl, about nine years old, who was peering at them from a half-open door off the living room. This was Isabel, the daughter of Mrs. Bannister and the deceased client. There seemed to be something wrong with the child. Her eyes looked haunted, like those of a ghost.

"It felt dangerous to be there. It felt exciting," Jennifer Bannister said as she led Alan toward a sofa.

The living room was huge and entirely white: white walls, white sofas, white tables, white shelves adorned with crystals. Alan sat down on a sofa with a small notebook propped on his knee. Mrs. Bannister was in her late thirties, beautiful but cold. An ice maiden. She wore a black suit, but whether because she was in mourning or because black suited her, it was hard to say. She closed her eyes in deep concentration. She smiled, visualizing the scene.

"Then the sprinklers came on—*pfff!*—all round us. And we *ran!*" Mrs. Bannister laughed to herself. "My . . . I remember that like it was yesterday . . . and . . . this was not long ago . . . we were watching Isabel in a school talent show. She was wonderful that night. I think Charles and I both felt what an amazing thing a family was. We felt it together, while she was up there on the stage. Oh, goodness . . ."

Jennifer Bannister opened her eyes. She was flushed with emotion. "Excuse me," she said, a little embarrassed.

Alan was busy writing down the scenes she had just described to remind himself to include those memories in the final cut of her husband's Zoe film. He looked up and put on the sympathetic expression he used with clients.

"I know it can be hard, Mrs. Bannister. But this is important. This is the foundation of the cutting process. I need you—your whole family—to help me choose the moments that you want to keep. I cannot do your husband justice without understanding him. Through you."

Out of the corner of his eye, Alan became aware that the daughter, Isabel, was still watching him, spying through the door. There was something in the little girl's eyes that bothered him. It wasn't just that she looked haunted—there was anger there, a piercing accusation that was unexpected from a child so young.

"I heard you were the best. That you'd know how to handle Charles," Mrs. Bannister told him. An uncomfortable tone had entered her voice. "My husband was a great man, Mr. Hakman. He deserves to be remembered as a great man."

Alan sensed an undertone, a subtext. He turned from Mrs. Bannister to the little girl, then back to the mother.

"After my initial cut, I will need to speak with Isabel," he said.

"Is that necessary?" Mrs. Bannister had just noticed the girl. She walked across the room, locked eyes briefly with her daughter, then shut the door. Without comment, she returned to her armchair.

Alan smiled, he hoped in a comforting manner. "There is nothing any of you can tell me that I will not know very soon," he said, choosing his words carefully.

"Of course. Yes," Mrs. Bannister agreed. Her expression gave nothing away. "Rom?" she called into the next room.

A Filipino butler appeared almost instantly. He was as perfect and unreadable as everything else in the strange house.

"Please call the Zoe Storage Lab," Mrs. Bannister said in the lofty tone rich people used with butlers. "Tell them Mr. Hakman will be dropping by."

"Very good, ma'am." The butler gave a small bow and left the room as silently as he had entered.

Jennifer Bannister returned her attention to Alan. She gave him a complicated look, one that was arrogant yet at the same time pleading. Alan was attuned to such subtleties. It was as if she was saying, *You'll be kind to me, won't you? I'm such a beautiful, helpless widow, after all . . . but if you're not nice, believe me, I'll tear you to shreds.* What she actually said, however, was: "Thank you. I've seen Rememories where the cutters were careless. They had no respect for the dead."

"The dead mean nothing to me, Mrs. Bannister," Alan told her. "I am taking this project because I respect the living."

The cold, lovely widow appeared to appreciate this sentiment. She nodded very slightly, indicating the interview was at an end.

SIX

Alan returned to the city from the Bannister estate and made his way by public transportation to the Zoe Implant Storage Lab, a gleaming white building in an expensive part of town near several municipal parks, an area of wide avenues and spacious vistas. Everything about the building gave off a sense of science and prosperity, the brave new world of technology and triumph that Eye Tech had created.

Inside, the lab was a metallic labyrinth of corridors. Alan waited at the Archive Front Desk while a female storage technician in a pale blue lab coat went down the long rows of the maze in search of his request. She came to a vault where she stopped to check her log.

Satisfied, she swung open the heavy metal door. The Zoe Implants were stored at human body temperature in protective containers inside the vault. It took the technician a few moments to locate the proper container, labeled CHARLES M. BANNISTER. She closed the vault and returned to the desk, where Alan stood waiting with his Chop Block laptop. He signed for the container, slipped the Zoe Implant into a special slot in his Chop Block, then carefully locked the case.

Alan left the lab bearing the heavy responsibility of possessing an entire lifetime in his hands: Charles M. Bannister, from the moment of his birth to his final heart attack, every nanosecond of existence, every sight he had ever seen. Who else but God had the opportunity to witness all the intimate details of another person's very being?

Alan had a premonition that the memories he carried in his Chop Block were some even God would rather not know about. But such thoughts didn't worry Alan. He had his reputation, after all. Alan Hakman: the cutter who never passed judgment, who took the dirty jobs others declined.

*   *   *

The invitation card, with its ornate gilt script on heavy paper, was as formal as the occasion it announced:

You are cordially invited to the Rememory of Daniel Monroe, in celebration of his life, on the 40th day of his passing.

5:30 to 7:30 at the Arlington Rememory Theater. Formal dress.

Like the Eye Tech lab, the Rememory Theater was the last word in architecture: all white curves and sleek surfaces, very expensive yet tasteful. Three security monitors kept watch on the guests as they arrived in the driveway and stepped from limousines in mourning gowns and suits of the finest quality. A Rememory, of course, was an elegant social event designed for the living more than for the dead, a chance for friends and relatives to gather. Unfortunately, a small group of protestors had congregated on the sidewalk, marring the splendor of the occasion. All the placards bore the same message:

DO NOT REWRITE HISTORY!
MEMORIES ARE SACRED!

Among the protestors were several tattooed men and women, strange individuals who tended to be angrier than the rest of the group. Their faces covered with colorful patterns, these people shouted at the arriving guests with what could only be described as religious fervor. A handful of security guards eyed them and the less vocal dissenters nervously, uncertain how explosive the situation might become.

Then Caroline Monroe, the wife of the deceased, arrived. As she exited her limousine, she was outraged to discover a protest in progress on the sidewalk outside her husband's Rememory.

"Why don't you people go home?" she screamed. "Just go home! Have some respect!"

When her words had no effect, she spat on the sidewalk in front of the protestors, raising more shouts from the tattooed fanatics. The scene was turning nastier. Finally, one of the security guards approached Caroline and put his arm firmly around her, drawing her into the theater.

"I'm sorry, Mrs. Monroe," he said. "We've never had a demonstration before."

This was not much comfort, but at last the widow turned from the protestors, mustered her dignity as best as she was able, and entered the theater, determined to make the best of the situation.

Guests kept arriving until the theater was packed, full of hushed, expectant voices.

There was excitement in the air. Daniel Monroe's Rememory was set to begin.

SEVEN

Alan arrived late and made his way immediately past the disturbance at the front of the building. Inside the theater he headed to the projection room at the rear of the auditorium. Jason Monroe, Daniel's brother, was waiting. Jason's long white hair flowed over the collar of his formal attire and he was nervous as a cat.

"Man, am I glad to see you!" he said.

"You would have had it sooner, but you didn't give me much time for such a complicated job," Alan told him.

Alan opened his Chop Block and popped out a Zoe Implant disk labeled D. MONROE—FINAL CUT. He slid the disk into the projection machine, then took a moment to gaze out a small window on the theater below. The rows of seats facing the large movie screen were quickly filling up as people found their places. Satisfied, Alan returned his attention to the projector. He pressed several buttons, making sure that the film was online and ready to go.

"Just hit play," Alan said.

"Good. Great." Jason glanced anxiously at his wristwatch. "Wow. Just in time. We need to rock and roll." He reached into his coat pocket, then handed an envelope to Alan, who accepted it without examining the payment inside.

"So that's it, huh?" Jason asked.

"That's it," Alan said.

Jason peered through the window of the projection room to see if he could start the Rememory. Alan left quietly just as the lights began to dim in the auditorium. The whispering and shuffling of the audience settled into an expectant silence as Alan circled to the back of the room. He drew a small notebook from his pocket and opened it as the film began.

· First there was only blackness. Then a tunnel of light as Danny's birth began to fill the screen. The audience sat in hushed wonder, staring up at the miracle of birth witnessed from the point of view of a baby, Danny himself coming into the world. Never in the history of mankind had memories such as this been available for view until Eye Tech's invention of the Zoe Implant.

The scene changed. Danny lay on the floor inside his house drawing with crayons, while his parents sat nearby watching TV. For Alan, this was better than any cinematic art, better than D. W. Griffith and Kubrick combined. This was reality, the essence of a languid childhood afternoon when time seemed to stretch out forever. As Danny continued to work, the audience gradually realized he was making a large black ant. He continued scribbling until . . . *snap!* The crayon broke because of too much pressure from his small hand.

With a shift of scene, Danny was outside in the backyard on a summer day, a family barbecue in progress. Burgers and hot dogs sizzled on the grill. All around milled family members of various ages.

Danny himself was no longer in his early childhood. His uncle Murray handed him a plate with a burger on it. Murray was a big, friendly man, a little sloppy in appearance but well-meaning.

"So, Danny, you still drawing?" Uncle Murray asked, bending down with a smile into the frame.

"Nope," said Danny simply, the answer of a child who hadn't yet learned to be polite.

"Didn'tcha wanna grow up to be an artist?" the grown-up persisted.

"Not anymore."

Uncle Murray grinned at the fickleness of kids. "Whaddya wanna do when you grow up?"

"I wanna be a doctor."

Murray made a show of reacting as if the answer was big news. "Doctor, eh? Clever kid. That'll keep you in the bucks. Why a doctor?"

"I wanna help people when they get hurt," Danny replied seriously.

Uncle Murray appeared simultaneously impressed and amused. "Awww, wouldja listen to this kid? You've got a good heart, Danny. That's all you need in life," he lied. "Now eat your burger."

Classical music welled up as the Rememory

continued, scene upon scene, year after year: the significant and well-edited moments of Daniel Monroe's lifetime, start to finish, minus anything unpleasant or unflattering to those left alive. An hour later, the Rememory was still in progress, and waiters outside the theater were setting up for the reception on the lawn. The group of protestors remained on the sidewalk, but they milled quietly because they had no one to harass. Meanwhile, the security monitors showed a tall man in his early thirties making his way across the lawn to the theater. This man was impeccably dressed in a dark suit.

"Good evening," he said crisply to a security guard, who allowed him to pass.

His name was Fletcher, and the guard, judging from the other man's clothes, assumed he belonged with the invited guests rather than with the scruffy protestors. This was as Fletcher had planned. He continued into the auditorium, slipping inside as the Monroe Rememory progressed.

On the screen, Danny, in his twenties, was attending a medical school class. A group of students gathered around a cadaver while a professor explained a specific procedure.

"We make the incision here," the professor said. "Hand me the number seventeen please."

But Danny had his own ideas and was not afraid to speak up. "Actually, Professor, I think the number twelve would be more appropriate."

The professor paused. A look of obvious irritation passed over his face. "Yes, correct, the number twelve. Thank you, Mr. Monroe."

The audience laughed and clapped in approval. This small moment captured the very essence of the Danny Monroe they knew and loved: yes, perhaps a little arrogant, but so smart you had to respect the guy, particularly when he was almost always right.

The scene changed. Danny listened in a hospital corridor while a patient's family thanked him profusely for his good work. He nodded politely, causing the frame to go up and down. Then his gaze shifted away from the family to the waiting area, where a young woman was seated on a chair. This was Caroline, his future wife, whom he was about to meet for the first time. From the way his gaze had settled upon her, it was obvious that he found her attractive. At last, he went over to her.

"Hello. I'm Dr. Daniel Monroe," he said smoothly. Did his tone hint at all the things to come: courtship, marriage, children, a long life together? The audience relished this pivotal moment in the life of the deceased.

On the screen, the young Caroline smiled. While in the auditorium, the older Caroline watched mesmerized, reliving the moment. It was the true magic of the Zoe Implant, to have such memories captured forever. Tears filled Caroline's eyes.

At the back of the theater, Alan stood, notebook in hand, and observed both the screening and the reaction of the audience. Rememories always stirred a wide variety of responses, and he was always curious to analyze what worked and what didn't. Some people were smiling, others frowned, and others, like Caroline Monroe, had tears in their eyes. Some hardly seemed to be paying attention at all, whispering to each other. Such was always the case, however; guests took the opportunity to socialize with people they hadn't seen for a while, and Alan didn't take their rudeness personally. All in all, he was satisfied with the success of his work.

Then Alan heard footsteps behind him.

Fletcher moved toward him through the shadows of the darkened auditorium.

"It's a strange profession you have, isn't it, Alan?" Fletcher said quietly. "You take people's lives and make lies out of them."

Alan gazed at the newcomer without expression. "Fletcher," he said. "It's been years."

"Eight years."

"I'm working," Alan told him. "I can't talk."

On the screen, an older Daniel Monroe stared at himself in the mirror of a men's clothing store.

"How can you handle it?" Fletcher asked unexpectedly. "People sleeping and shitting. People stealing from each other, manipulating each other. The obscenity."

From the seats, a woman hushed him. Seeing that a confrontation was unavoidable, Alan discreetly led Fletcher to the back of the room. "I don't have time to catch up."

"Well, I'm hurt. But that's not why I'm here."

"I'm booked solid for the next two months."

Fletcher smiled thinly. "No, no, no, I don't have a job lead for you. Actually, you have something that I need. I know you've taken the Bannister project. I want it."

Alan gave Fletcher a questioning look. "I thought you didn't cut anymore?"

"I'm offering you five hundred thousand dollars in cash."

Alan said nothing, but his expression showed both disapproval and distaste.

"Oh, what? The Code?" Fletcher said sarcastically. "Would you forget the damn Code and grow up. This is real life now."

From behind them in the auditorium, Alan heard the Rememory ending. As the lights slowly came on, the roar of applause drowned out a surge of classical music. People smiled broadly, and others were overcome by emotion. Jason Monroe joined Alan and Fletcher. Fletcher politely took a step away to give Alan time with his client, but he remained within earshot.

"Hey, did you change the color of our fishing boat?" Jason asked.

"No," Alan told him.

"Are you sure? 'Cause the way I remember it, it was green, not red. Weird. Like all my memories in that boat have it being *green*. It's a total mind fuck."

"Maybe it was green," Alan told him without interest, simply to put an end to the conversation. He picked up his Chop Block, which was resting on the floor by his side. "I do need to go."

"Okay, rush, rush, rush," Jason said agreeably. "Beautiful work. I'll keep you in mind for me."

Jason left the building, heading toward the reception outside. All around, people were exiting in groups, talking among themselves.

"Ah, yes, the questions," Fletcher, suddenly back at Alan's side, said. " 'I remembered it different!' 'Are you sure that's what happened?' "

Alan faced the younger man. "Some of us still live by the Code, Fletcher. Some of us didn't walk away. We have what it takes."

Fletcher appeared amused. "What *does* it take? Delusion? Obsession? Guilt? No, I don't have those. Not as much as you do." He paused, then continued in a more conciliatory tone, "I'm asking you to think it over. Five hundred grand. Consider it. I'll be in touch."

Without another word, Fletcher strode from the building. Alone, Alan sighed, not happy with the encounter. He sensed that Fletcher could be a problem. He followed a moment later, walking out onto the lawn, where a group of musicians played polite background music and waiters bearing cocktails circulated among the guests. Alan passed through the crowd to say good-bye to Caroline Monroe.

"He was such a good father, too," a woman was saying. "When his son had the mumps—oh, my God, my heart was in my throat!"

"And that part with his partners!" said a man. "Could you believe those guys? They got what they deserved!"

"We're gonna miss him," the woman said.

Would they? Alan wasn't so sure. But that was beyond the boundaries of his job. He continued scanning the crowd until he spotted Caroline close to the bar. She was talking to her best friend, Natalie, an attractive woman who looked a good deal younger than her years.

"It's the Rememory your husband deserved, Caroline," Natalie was saying as Alan approached. "He really was something special."

When Alan approached the women, shame passed across Natalie's face. Alan, in his Godlike role of cutter, knew very well what her reaction signified. Scene 241-R, deleted forever, but not before Alan had seen it: a bedroom at night, Natalie moaning in ecstasy as Danny Monroe made passionate love to her. "Oh, Danny, fuck me you pig!" she had screamed.

Natalie lowered her eyes, but she didn't need to worry. After decades of being a cutter, Alan was immune to moral judgments. He had come across such infidelities and worse. He simply accepted human imperfection as part of the job.

Caroline Monroe turned and said hello with a smile. She pointed at the protestors still gathered on the sidewalk beyond the reception area. "Mr. Hakman, why are they tattooed like that?"

Alan's eyes moved across the tattooed faces at the far side of the lawn. There were only a half dozen of them left, but they bothered him on a visceral level. He didn't understand the anti-Zoe fervor sweeping the country. It seemed to Alan irrational, a viewpoint that was beyond his ability to understand.

"I'm not sure," he answered truthfully.

"Oh, they look so . . . *grotesque*," Caroline said.

Alan nodded curtly, feeling an overwhelming desire to get away. "Good day, Mrs. Monroe," he said and walked off across the lawn, his Chop Block in hand.

"Hey! Look, it's the butcher!" someone called as he walked through the gate to the street. The tattooed protestors quickly gathered around him.

"Butcher!" they screamed. "Monster!"

Alan refused to speed up. He showed no sign of hearing the insults, not even when one of the protestors hurled his placard at Alan and hit him on the back. Fortunately, one of the security guards came out to keep the protestors at bay, allowing Alan to get away. But Alan didn't appear to notice his rescue either.

Alan was a man beyond the reach of human emotions. It was marvelous the way he just kept on walking. Untouched. Undisturbed. Totally alone.

EIGHT

For Alan Hakman, only the past filtered through the numb barricade of his solitary state. Only the past had the power to hurt him. . . .

That day forty-two years ago, with the sun shining in an unnatural sky of metallic blue, he and Louis had battled with wooden sticks as imaginary swords in the unfinished building. They had climbed all the way to the fifth floor, high above the street. All these years later, Alan could recall the exact smell of damp concrete and musty sawdust and the play of light and shadow filtering through the empty windows and unfinished walls.

Alan was the leader of the two, the aggressive one. It seemed almost a natural law in a situation like this: two boys playing in an empty building, one urging the other along, the second following the stronger's lead. When Alan got bored playing at swords, he took his stick and ducked around a corner out of Louis's sight.

"Hey, Louis!" he shouted. "Look what's over here!"

Without enthusiasm, Louis followed Alan around the corner, trying his best to appear bold and brave like Alan, but obviously intimidated by the dangerous place where they played. He found Alan standing at the edge of a great chasm. There was a gaping hole that dropped down five stories to the ground below. It was impossible to say what would fill this hole eventually but in the meantime a wooden plank had been positioned across the gap, bridging the two sides of the unfinished floor. It was a perilous spot even to stand, and the bridge worse still, with nothing other than gravity holding the plank in place.

Alan turned to Louis and grinned. The unfinished building with its many hazards appealed to his imagination. Alan threw his stick down into the hole. It tumbled down . . . down through the empty space until at last it clattered on a pile of rubble far below. Even the echo of the distant sound the stick made as it hit the ground was intriguing.

Standing well back from the gaping hole, Louis anxiously took off his glasses and cleaned them roughly on his shirt. It was a nervous tic he had, but it did not help him see the dangers at hand any more clearly.

Would Alan have acted differently today? Would he have noticed how Louis, doing his best to act brave, was in fact nearly paralyzed with terror?

But Alan didn't notice his new friend's terror. He felt only the adrenaline of the new experience—the adventure in a place he knew deep down he shouldn't be. . . .

An electronic humming filled Alan's apartment, the pulsing sound of his Guillotine warming up. It was night; the city outside was sleeping, giving Alan the feeling of being marooned on an island of his own making, entirely separate from anything but the work at hand. Night was a good time for cutting.

He slid his Chop Block into its place in the Guillotine. The Zoe Implant glowed briefly through the Chop Block while the Guillotine announced itself: *Receiving Zoe footage—Charles Bannister.*

A series of electronic sounds burst out of the Guillotine as all the monitors sprang to life. *Processing and sorting footage,* the computer said in its toneless drone.

Suddenly the monitors were flooded with images of Bannister eating, sleeping, shitting, writing, making love, running, working, swimming. The smallest of the monitors was deluged with columns of numbers, scrolling down and cross-referencing. Alan methodically checked this information against the images on the monitors until he was content that everything was working properly.

He pulled another monitor closer to him so he could see better. On this screen, there was a list of categories that the individual moments of Bannister's life would be stored under, each category flashing as another image was shuffled its way:

- SLEEP
- FOOD CONSUMPTION
- WORK
- CHILDHOOD
- SEX

- RECREATION
- EXERCISE
- TRAUMA
- PUBERTY

And on and on, dozens and dozens more. Alan sat back in his work chair and explored the clutter of sights and sounds as the Guillotine began its long job of putting every moment in its proper place. The technology was advanced, but even the quickest computer had its work set out for it, arranging and rearranging every second of a man's existence. Engrossed in his job, Alan hardly noticed the time passing. He worked until nearly dawn, slept a few hours, then got up and immediately returned to the Guillotine. This first part of the process would take several days.

Spread out on the console were notebooks, photo albums, newspaper clippings, and sources other than the Zoe Implant to help him with the editing of Charles Bannister's life. The limitation of the Zoe Implant was that it was entirely subjective; every moment was seen, of course, from the carrier's eyes. To organize such a mass of material, the cutter occasionally needed an objective viewpoint. So while the monitors continued to run, Alan sat back in his editing chair and studied the newspaper clippings before him.

A famous man in his day, Bannister had frequently been in the news. Such information was always a lucky break for a cutter trying to get a grip on the overall picture. In one newspaper supplement, Mr. and Mrs. Bannister beamed out from a picture of them in their luxurious mansion. Headlines screamed out from articles and interviews:

CHARLES BANNISTER,
EYE TECH ATTORNEY,
DIES OF HEART COMPLICATIONS

STAR ATTORNEY VICTORIOUS
IN SOLOMON V. EYE TECH CASE

BANNISTER PROCLAIMS EYE TECH
"A PROFOUND PUBLIC SERVICE"

After a while, Alan turned his attention back to the Guillotine, and he began the long job of cutting, pasting, and rearranging moments from Bannister's life. All the while, he took notes on what he was watching. Later in the afternoon, he began flipping through a music catalog to begin his consideration of the appropriate accompaniment. This orchestration was also part of his craft, a way to bridge scenes and emphasize significant emotional moments. Alan generally preferred classical music for his Zoe films; he believed that classical strains lent a certain amount of dignity to the finished product, though occasionally he allowed jazz and even honky-tonk piano for lighter moments. In the case of Charles Bannister, Alan thought that Beethoven would be suitable—perhaps some excerpts from various symphonies and the late string quartets.

As he worked, Alan occasionally glanced at the monitors to see, through Bannister's eyes, various Eye Tech contracts, documents, memos, and design proposals. To be dealing with a life that was concerned with his own profession was new to Alan. As the primary Eye Tech attorney, Bannister had known all the trade secrets of the Zoe Implant, and Alan found himself learning those secrets, too. Alan had little doubt that such confidential information was the reason Fletcher had offered him five hundred grand to take the Bannister project off his hands. For Alan, however, the Code was an essential part of the cutter's trade, and the money didn't tempt him. As far as he was concerned, he would guard Bannister's secrets to the grave, just as he would for any other client—even Danny Monroe, for instance, with his seedy sexual affairs.

Close to midnight, Alan came to a scene that set off an inner alarm. He pressed a button and played the scene again at normal speed.

The monitor showed the Bannister house, which had become familiar to him. At the bottom right-hand corner, the display read:

C. BANNISTER: 50 YEARS: 175 DAYS: 18 HOURS

Charles Bannister peeked into his daughter's darkened bedroom from the hall. Light from the corridor spilled in; the little girl lay in bed, surrounded by her stuffed animals and dolls.

"Hi, baby. You still awake?" Bannister called softly.

"No," Isabel said and rolled onto her side.

Charles came in and sat down on her bed.

"Daddy loves you so much—you know that?"

"Yes. I love you, too," the little girl answered.

Charles bent forward and kissed her on the forehead. They were both silent for a moment. There was an awkward tension between them.

"Do you want to come down to my study? I'd like to show you what I'm working on," Charles said after a moment.

Isabel raised her head from the pillow. "What are you working on?"

"A new case. Come on."

Charles peeled the sheet off his daughter and hoisted her onto his back. He carried her out of the bedroom and down the stairs. His office was a richly appointed room lined with books and oak furniture. Charles set Isabel down on the carpet; then he closed and locked the door behind.

"Daddy?"

"Yes, sweetie?"

"I want to go to sleep."

"In a little while, baby," Charles said, moving toward her. "In a little while . . ."

Alan watched the scene for several more

minutes until he came to its inevitable conclusion. Of all the terrible things he had witnessed, this was certainly one of the more terrible. But, as always, he was not there to judge; he had come to that conclusion a long time before. Cutters either went crazy watching the uncensored truths of clients' lives, or they learned to take a detached attitude. Alan's face betrayed no emotion as he observed Charles Bannister in the room with his daughter. When the scene was finished, Alan typed in a series of commands; then he hit the DELETE button.

As the audio rewound, he pulled one of the monitors closer to him. It was labeled FINISHED SCENES. He hit a few more buttons and finished with stroking PLAY SCENE.

On the monitor, Charles Bannister was once again in the hallway peeking into his daughter's bedroom through the open door.

"Hi, baby. You still awake?" he asked.

"No," she told him, just as definitely as before.

Undeterred, Charles walked in and sat down on Isabel's bed.

"Daddy loves you so much—you know that?"

"Yes. I love you, too," she answered.

Once again, Charles bent over to kiss the child on the forehead. But now there was no awkward silence between them, no tension. Instead, the scene cut smoothly to a very nice moment at a crowded school theater at night. The display at the button on the screen read:

C. BANNISTER: 50 YEARS: 176 DAYS: 19 HOURS

On the monitor, Charles watched from the audience as Isabel stood on the stage in an elementary school production. She spoke loudly, without a trace of stage fright: ". . . a good night to all, and to all a good night!"

As the curtain fell, the audience stood and erupted into applause. Charles clapped the loudest of all, a perfect father. He turned to his wife, Jennifer, standing beside him.

"She was wonderful!" Charles said enthusiastically.

The two parents glowed with pride as the curtain opened again and the cast of children in Christmas costumes took their bows. Alan pressed the PAUSE button, freezing the frame on this happy family scene.

Was deleting the unpleasantness that had occurred on the office floor the truth? No, of course not. Alan didn't fool himself. But he thought of himself as an artist. Just as the mortician used makeup to tidy up a deceased face, Alan had his little tricks to erase disease and human difficulties.

The final cut showed life as it should have been rather than life as it was. Cutting was an art, and Alan Hakman its proudest practitioner.

NINE

An hour later, Alan was still editing and making notes. When he looked up with bleary eyes, he saw there was a party in progress at the Bannister mansion. The name and age display read:

C. BANNISTER: 52 YEARS: 255 DAYS:
23 HOURS

On the screen, Charles Bannister was walking through a crowd of well-dressed guests making small talk and sipping wine in his living room: a typical gathering at an expensive suburban home, with everybody smiling politely and pretending to be the best of friends. Bannister's wife came up beside him; he stopped for a moment to kiss her affectionately on the neck. Jennifer Bannister, the perfect hostess, was beautiful and beguiling, flawlessly dressed, not a hair out of place. As a couple, Charles and Jennifer had their act down. No one outside those in Alan's profession would suspect the darker secrets of the Bannisters' lives.

Alan was watching idly when in the background, beyond Jennifer Bannister's neck, he caught sight of a man with thick glasses in a wheelchair. The man was obviously by himself, left out of the general merriment. Awkwardly, as though for something to do, he picked up a framed photograph of Isabel from a bureau and began to study it. The thick glasses, the face—there was something oddly familiar about the man. Alan stared at the monitor, feeling as though a trapdoor had just opened up beneath his stomach. But he still wasn't sure—there had to be some mistake. He continued to watch as Bannister walked over to the man.

"She wanted to stay up and say hello, but the poor thing fell asleep," Charles said, speaking about his daughter in his most pleasantly innocuous party voice.

"It's a very beautiful picture," the man in the wheelchair replied. "She's a very bright little girl."

Then, as Alan hardly dared to breathe, the man removed his thick glasses and cleaned them roughly on his shirt. Alan stabbed at the PAUSE button with a trembling hand, causing the scene to freeze. On the monitor, the man's face wasn't entirely clear, so Alan used a dial to adjust the focus, causing his features to sharpen. With a shock, Alan recognized the man. There couldn't be any mistake about it. Alan pressed another button, which made the scene progress at half-speed. He watched in slow motion as the man continued to clean his glasses. It was Louis, his new friend from that terrible day so many years ago.

But it was impossible. It simply couldn't be!

Alan and Louis . . . the memory was like a whirlpool, engulfing Alan: the two boys on the fifth floor of the unfinished building, standing in front of the gaping hole in the floor—a hole that was a stomach-lurching abyss, nothing but dust and emptiness all the way down to the hard ground five floors below. Forty-two years ago, Alan and Louis had stood together at that fatal spot, daring each other to look over the edge.

"Let's go back down," Louis had said, trying his best to keep up a tone of bravado, as if he were getting bored. But his tone betrayed him. He *really* wanted to get away from that hellish place!

So Louis turned, made a kind of funny face, and began to walk down the concrete stairs. But Alan remained by the plank bridge that lay across the gaping hole. The bridge was curiously inviting to Alan, a special passage from one side of the floor to another—a dangerous passage, certainly, but obviously the workmen had used the plank for a walkway or it wouldn't be there. If big, clumsy adults walked here, why couldn't Alan?

Tentatively, Alan put one foot on the plank and shook it. The bridge made a wobbly sound—*rattle, rattle, rattle* echoed through the building. Yet the plank seemed sturdy enough, at least if a person was careful. After a long moment, Alan, with a wondrous sense of the absolute emptiness beneath him, stepped out on the plank. He was so frightened he could barely breathe. At the same time, he felt more alive than he had ever felt in the nine years of his life.

"Don't!" Louis cautioned. He hadn't gone downstairs after all. Mesmerized and terrified, he had turned to watch what Alan was doing.

Daring himself, Alan took two fast steps across the bridge. He was committed—no turning back. Clouds of dust puffed up from the plank and hung in the air. Halfway across the plank, Alan paused to collect himself. Testing his balance, he gazed up through a hole in the ceiling, where he was able to see the sky clear and beautiful overhead. Birds circled high above him.

Alan felt enormously calm, yet at the same time exhilarated. It was like he was immortal. Casually, he looked back over his shoulder to enjoy Louis's admiration. The other boy stared at him, his hand over his mouth. Quickly, Alan walked the final steps across the bridge and jumped off safely on the other side.

He knew he was showing off. He liked Louis, but by nature he was competitive. Louis's timidity made Alan's courage seem bolder and more admirable in his own eyes.

"See?" he called to Louis, moving away from the edge. He kept his tone modest, adding an aura of steely calm to his accomplishment. "Wasn't so bad. Come on."

Louis looked positively sick. "No. No, I can't."

"It's easy. Just don't look down."

Very cautiously, Louis moved to the edge and glanced over into the abyss. He stepped backward immediately, shaking his head.

"Louis!" Alan said despairingly.

Alan's tone was enough to make Louis try again. Slowly, the timid boy forced himself to approach the bridge. Very tentatively, he took a step onto it.

"See, it's steady," Alan called from the far side.

Louis took another step; the plank shook and wobbled. He put his arms out for balance and very carefully began to walk across the gaping hole, one foot after the other. But two-thirds of the way across, he stopped, unable to continue.

"Come on," Alan encouraged.

"No, I can't move." Louis tried to go back to where he had started. But the bridge began to rattle more seriously, and he was again paralyzed with fear.

"I can't move," Louis said in a pitiful voice.

Alan realized too late what a truly serious situation they were in. The blood had drained out of Louis's face. He breathed in shallow bursts.

"Okay. You're almost there," Alan said in a very different tone, no longer taunting. He wanted nothing more than to get Louis off the plank. "Just a few more steps."

Realizing he couldn't remain two-thirds of the way across the plank, Louis tried to move forward, but terror made him clumsy. His foot slipped. He stumbled and fell from the plank. Somehow he was able to lunge forward and grab hold of the edge of the fifth floor.

Alan watched helplessly as Louis made a final effort to hang on to the edge. Frantically, Louis tried to pull himself up. But his hands slipped in the dust, and his body slid down. Louis's face was red with panic, horrible to see. For one brief instant, his eyes filled with bitter accusation: *You made me do this. It's all your fault!* The entire struggle took only a few seconds; then, with an awful scream, he fell backward.

There was a crash of debris far below as Louis hit the ground. The sound echoed in the hollow shell of the building, then slowly died until there was only silence, which was more horrible still. Alan stood stock-still, unable to believe what had just happened. Slowly, he forced himself to the edge and looked down, hoping that, by some miracle, Louis would be standing up laughing. But there was no miracle. Louis lay five floors below, his body crushed, broken, and still. Something closer at hand attracted Alan's attention: an ivory talisman on a leather hoop that had caught on a twisted nail jutting from the ledge. The talisman had been around Louis's neck. Without thinking why, Alan reached down and plucked it from the nail.

Then he ran. Overwhelmed with guilt and horror, Alan rushed down the five flights of stairs all the way to the bottom, careening around corners, slipping and sliding . . . around and around until at last he reached the ground floor. Mustering up all his courage, Alan approached the place where Louis lay at an unnatural angle on the rubble. Alan inched his way closer until he was standing directly over his new friend. It was only then that he noticed blood spreading over the concrete.

It was horrendous! He was *standing* in Louis's blood! Alan jumped back and tried to scrape his shoes clean on the concrete. All he could think about was kicking up dirt over his footprints, making it look as if he had never been there. He hardly knew what he was doing anymore. He scraped his shoes and kicked dirt as if he were doing a crazy dance. Then he turned and fled, frantically making his way out of the construction site. To his nine-year-old mind, the passages seemed labyrinthine . . . until at last he was out in the light of day, dashing through the streets of the town, with tears streaming down his face.

In his memory, he ran and ran until he saw his mother and father standing with an old woman in the doorway of a house. He hurried toward them across a street, oblivious to the traffic. A car screeched to a halt just before hitting him, but such a fate seemed inconsequential after what had happened to Louis. At last, Alan came up to his parents, breathing hard, incoherent with shock.

"Alan, where have you been?" his father asked with concern.

"Why are you crying?" his mother demanded. "Is something the matter?"

Alan stared up at his parents' eyes. He was safe, and the incident in the half-finished building was already receding into the realm of dreams. Part of him wanted to tell his parents the truth about the horrible thing that had happened. He suspected even then, at this childhood moment, that the truth would set him free. It would be difficult to say, certainly, but then the guilt and fear would go away. A lie, on the other hand, would last forever. He struggled within himself while he caught his breath. Standing above him, his parents seemed so tall and distant. In the end, he simply could not get the truthful words out.

"No. Nothing," he said quickly to his parents. "I . . . I just thought you had left without me."

"Ha! That's not a bad idea," his father said, his idea of being funny.

"Oh, stop it," said his mother. "What do you have in your hand?"

Mrs. Hakman reached down and made

Alan unclench his fist. Louis's ivory talisman was still in his sweaty palm. He hadn't meant to bring it with him from the building; he had simply forgotten to throw it away. A new fear overwhelmed him. How could he explain the necklace to his mother? He was caught, he was sure. Caught red-handed with evidence of his crime.

"Did you find this?" his mother asked solemnly.

Numbly, Alan managed to nod.

"It's nice," she said. "Here . . ." She tied the talisman around Alan's neck. He marked this moment forever in his mind, knowing the talisman would remind him always of what he had done.

Finally, the family drove away in their car. In the backseat, Alan turned and stared out the rear window as the construction site, looming silent and alone, gradually disappeared from view.

TEN

Alan walked from his apartment to Thelma's along the narrow streets of the nighttime city. The streets were vaguely sinister to him, like something from a nightmare. His mind was in turmoil, too restless to settle on any one thing. Near Thelma's building, he passed a wall that was plastered with dozens of posters advertising Zoe Implants. Many of the posters were scrawled full of anti-Zoe graffiti, which caught Alan's attention. One advertisement read:

EYE TECH—POSTCARDS FROM THE PAST

But beneath this, someone had written with spray paint:

REMEMBER FOR YOURSELF

It astonished Alan how the technology had polarized the country, one more cultural divide to make people hate one another. He saw the subject, of course, from his own experience. For Alan, the implants enhanced human existence. Life was so fleeting, after all. Wasn't it a blessing to capture human moments so they might endure for all time? Those instances would be artfully arranged, of course, so they added up to something meaningful, a narrative rather than the mere chaos of random events.

Deep in thought, Alan climbed the stairs to Thelma's apartment. On the landing outside her door, he heard a girl's voice saying adamantly, in a grating voice, "But I don't *want* to go!" Alan recognized it for what it was: a Guillotine loop.

He knocked on the door of apartment six. Above the sound of the Guillotine loop, he could hear Thelma and her assistant, Michael, in the middle of a loud argument. The girl on the loop kept saying the same thing again and again: "But I don't *want* to go! . . . But I don't *want* to go! . . . But I don't *want* to go!" And all the time, Thelma and Michael continued to squabble. Their spat set Alan's teeth on edge.

While he waited for someone to answer his knock, footsteps approached from inside. There was a pause; then at last the door opened. Michael stared at Alan with hostility. Surprisingly, he was nursing a black eye and there was a bandage on his cheek.

"Alan," Michael said without emotion. "You look like shit. Come in."

"What happened to your face?"

"I'd rather not elaborate."

Alan entered the apartment and closed the door behind him. In contrast to his own sterile workplace, Thelma's apartment was a cozy mess. He couldn't imagine how she could live that way. The place looked like a hurricane had come through. The paint was cracking and unclean. Every surface was piled high with newspapers, empty Chinese food boxes, coffee cups, and scattered clothes. A number of Russian movie posters hung haphazardly on the walls.

At the far end of this chaos, Thelma sat at an editing console, watching a group of teenagers on the main monitor. The teenagers, dressed in Halloween costumes, stood in front of the headlights of a parked car. On the other monitors there were various scenes from the Zoe being edited. The name and age display read:

N. CALDWELL: 15 YEARS: 316 DAYS:
23 HOURS

"But I don't *want* to go!" the teenage girl complained one more time.

Thelma rewound the clip, then paused it. She stood up and rubbed her eyes; she'd spent too many hours at the console. She wore a brightly colored housedress, inelegant but comfortable. "So you still don't believe me?" she said, turning to Michael.

"I just think it's false. Completely false," her scrawny young assistant answered heatedly. "You've decided that this scene, this event, is what made this woman who she was. You've turned this woman's entire life into a straight line drawn from this particular moment! How can you make a decision like that, boiling a life down to one—"

"It's a decision you have to make," Thelma interrupted, just as heatedly. "The Zoe Implant presents us with a complete life, with all its complexities, nuances, and randomness. We have to make story decisions. Otherwise there will be no Rememory."

Michael shook his head. "Yeah, yeah, okay," he said disagreeably. "I still don't buy it."

"You don't have to buy it. Just do it and trust me." Thelma sighed. When she spoke again, her voice brightened slightly, but still had its barbs. "Alan darling, you look spooked. Sorry about the place. The kid's a mess."

"Thelma, I need to talk to you. Alone."

Thelma didn't appear pleased to take on any more problems. She studied Alan with a mixture of exasperation and curiosity. After a moment, she said, "Michael honey, run down to the store and buy us some cigarettes."

"We've got eight packs already," he told her sullenly.

"Then you go return 'em, sweetheart. We don't need that many," Thelma said without a change of tone. Alan watched as she gave him a light kiss. With a lick of her thumb, she ironed down the edge of his bandage. Very motherly.

Michael glanced back and forth from

Thelma to Alan, getting the picture. Ungraciously, he put on his jacket and left, slamming the door behind him.

"He's an emotional one," Thelma said. She sat down on the couch and pushed aside clothes and papers. "You all right?"

"I saw Fletcher yesterday," Alan said.

Thelma's expression became more guarded. "Really?"

"What happened to him since he quit? He seems changed."

"Fletcher," she said. For a moment her eyes lost their focus and she seemed far away. "Now he was a great assistant. For the first few years we stayed in touch. Then his sister, Laura—you remember Laura? Well, her son died of leukemia. He was twelve. She never got over it. Refused to even have his Zoe footage edited. She'd been watching his entire life through since he died. Didn't speak, barely ate. Just stared. I don't think she knew who Fletcher was anymore. After that, he dropped off the map completely."

Alan took the crumpled red flyer out of his pocket and handed it to her. "Do you think he could be involved with the anti-implant groups?"

Thelma lit a cigarette and considered the question. "I've heard rumors, talk of them being organized by an ex-cutter," she said, blowing out smoke. "I never thought it could be Fletcher."

"He wants to buy Bannister's footage," Alan told her.

Without a word, Thelma led the way into her kitchen, indicating that Alan was to follow. The kitchen was even messier than the rest of the apartment. There were dirty dishes in the sink and more open containers of food. A newspaper was spread out on the kitchen table next to an overflowing ashtray. The headline read:

FREAK FIRE ENGULFS
EYE TECH FACTORY, 3 DEAD

Alan sat at the table and took a moment to read the story. The front page had a black-and-white photograph of a burning factory. The story below suggested the blaze was most likely an accident, but the arson squad was investigating. All the facts weren't in yet.

"This is yesterday's paper," Thelma said. "They've become like religious fanatics. A group of them gave Michael one hell of a beating last night. It's not just talk anymore." Smoking and watching Alan read the article, she sat across from him at the table. "If they're after Bannister, the bastard isn't worth fighting for. Give his footage back to his widow. Let her deal with it."

Alan looked up. "I can't give it back. I saw someone in that project that I haven't seen for years."

"I hate it when that happens."

"He's at a party," Alan continued, "in a crowd. He's never mentioned by name. I need to find him, but he's not a main character. It will take days for the Guillotine to track him through the footage."

Thelma appeared curious, as though she couldn't imagine Alan Hakman with a personal life, an actual friend outside his obsessive dedication to his job. "Who is this person?"

Alan kept it vague. "Someone . . . from when I was a kid. Bannister's life is my only lead."

She shrugged. "Then go through Bannister's family. Snoop around. Tell them you're researching the project. It might be faster than waiting for the Guillotine track."

A black-and-white framed photograph on a nearby shelf caught Alan's attention. The young dancer rehearsed before a wall-length mirror. She was very pretty. Alan picked up the frame and immediately the picture began to move. Such picture loops had become popular in recent years, both in advertising and for the home. Alan watched as the girl danced beautifully for ten seconds; then the loop began again. There was something very captivating about the innocence and grace of the woman in the photo.

Thelma smiled. "Michael just got that framed for me. It's from the first life I ever cut. Eleanor Wilson. Remember, they were silent back then. And shorter. Only recorded peak moments on and off during a life. But there was beauty to it, Alan. Not like today, with sound, color. It's too real now. It feels too much like life. It frightens me."

Without another word, Alan departed.

"Be careful," Thelma called after him as he went out the door. Alone, she picked up the picture Alan had been fondling and watched the dancer go through her brief routine. For Thelma, the black-and-white image brought back the old days of idealism when the life of a cutter seemed simpler, when one didn't need to be so careful about clients and currents. With a sigh, she cleaned the glass against her housedress, then set the frame back on her musty shelf.

ELEVEN

Delila's bookstore wasn't far from Thelma's apartment, only a few blocks. Alan wasn't certain what sort of reception he would get after their last . . . what? Quarrel? Miscommunication? However he tried to define the last incident they'd had, their relationship was as good as dead. He wasn't sure why, but Delila and he saw life from such different angles they might as well have come from different planets.

Alan entered the bookstore; as always, he felt happy just to be there. He loved the snug disorder of all the rare and used books crowded on every shelf. He saw Delila before she noticed him. She was sitting on the floor near the back of the store surrounded by piles of books, busy arranging them in stacks. It was astonishing how lovely she was. Everything about her was graceful, intelligent, and familiar. He would have been happy simply to stare at her for the rest of the evening.

Delila, sensing his presence, stared at him briefly without a word or change of expression. Then she continued her sorting and arranging until her nerves betrayed her and she accidentally knocked over one of the piles of books.

Alan squatted down and tried to help her pick them up.

"Don't," she said tensely. "Just leave them."

He handed her one of the fallen books and stepped back. "It's the new project, Delila. I've found something on it, something important. I just need to dig a little bit."

"A new cutting job? Is *that* what you're talking about?" Her tone was incredulous. "Alan, you've seen so much living, and somehow you missed the point completely. There's no place for me with you. You haven't even made room for yourself."

"I can't do it without you," he said simply.

She glared angrily. "I'm sorry, Alan. You should go."

It was no use. Maybe time would help his cause, but at just that moment, there was nothing he could do or say. He lowered his head, defeated, and went to the door, waiting for her to call him back and grant their love a reprieve.

Delila hesitated, as though about to speak or change her mind. But whatever she might have said remained unspoken. The shop door closed with its friendly tinkle and he was gone.

The following day, Alan set up the Guillotine in his apartment to search for further scenes between Charles Bannister and the man with the thick glasses in the wheelchair: Louis, the child from that terrible afternoon who had somehow survived his devastating fall. Clearly, Bannister knew Louis well enough to invite him to the party. So it was a matter of finding the moment of their meeting, which wouldn't be easy to sort out from the volume of information contained in Bannister's Zoe Implant.

Alan set a frozen image of Louis's face from the party on one monitor, while a second monitor scanned footage of Bannister's life, comparing and searching for a match. As the Guillotine set to work, Alan waited, fully aware that this process could take several days.

Alan really didn't know what to think. He kept remembering how he had stood near the plank bridge in the unfinished building, gazing in horror at Louis's body lying still and broken five stories below. More conclusive still, he had run down to the ground floor and stood in Louis's blood—actually *stood* in the blood, getting the fluid all over his shoes! How then could Louis appear as an adult in Bannister's Zoe memories? It didn't make any sense. After a while, Alan left the Guillotine to its seemingly endless search and went out.

Fletcher had called earlier that morning to say Alan and he needed to talk. Alan had agreed to meet the other man in a public place, a crowded subway station not far from Alan's apartment. He didn't trust Fletcher enough to be alone with him.

A light drizzle was falling from an unfriendly gray sky as Alan headed to the subway. Alan fought against the rush hour crowd exiting the subway. He bought a token and made his way to the express train platform. Dead in the middle of the station, he hoped he would be safe. The subway was a world unto itself, an underground universe that was dimly lit and unpleasant to smell. When he arrived, he found Fletcher sitting on a bench with people rushing all around him.

"I'm here," Alan said, coming up from behind the other man.

Fletcher turned to find Alan on the opposite side of a metal fence. Alan was on the downtown side, Fletcher on the uptown side. Alan sat with his back to Fletcher on his side of the divide.

"Is this why you wanted to meet here?" Fletcher asked.

"I feel safer like this," Alan answered.

"How's Thelma doing?"

"Well."

Fletcher smiled. "God, that old kook! She'd always say, 'The closest distance between any two shots is a dissolve.' "

Alan wasn't much in the mood for small talk, so he got right to the point. "I can't give you Bannister. You know I can't."

Fletcher didn't conceal his disappointment. He watched as a train pulled into the station and a mass of people passed through the doors.

"It's unbelievable when you think about it," Fletcher remarked. "One in twenty of these people has an implant."

Fletcher watched as a young woman pushed a baby stroller past his bench. He continued watching as mother and stroller moved down the platform.

"How will that baby remember his mother years from now?" he asked. "Will he remember the special moments between them or the moments someone like you decides are special."

"My job is to help people remember the way they want to remember," Alan replied.

Fletcher smiled skeptically. "Noble," he said. "But you don't understand the scope of the damage. There is no way to measure the profound effect the Zoe Implant has had on the way people relate to each other. 'Am I being filmed?' 'Should I say this or not?' 'What will they think in thirty years if I do this or that?' And what about the simple right not to be photographed? The right not to pop up in some guy's Rememory without even knowing you were being filmed?"

Alan, of course, had heard all these arguments before. "Look," he said, "I didn't invent this technology. People must want this technology or they wouldn't buy it. It fulfills a human need."

Fletcher gave a slight nod to a young man near him on his side of the platform. This was Simon; he had come with Fletcher to the meeting in case more than words were needed to convince Alan to hand over the Bannister project. Simon had a faint tattoo on the side of his face, the mark of an anti-Zoe protestor.

Fletcher glanced away, hoping that Simon would not be necessary. "Alan," he said, "you take murderers and make them saints. That's why we need Charles Bannister. He was a public figure for Eye Tech, their star attorney. Well-respected. Loved his family. Gave to charity. And if *you* get through with him, that's all anyone will know. But . . . Bannister is the first Eye Tech employee whose implant has left the confines of the corporation. His widow fought for that. It doesn't take a genius to assume that she has something to hide. And Bannister oversaw all their corporate dealings. Every memo, blueprint, and contract passed before his eyes. We know that Eye Tech's hands aren't clean. Bannister's chip is evidence."

Alan shook his head. "You want to fight Eye Tech with a scandal?"

"The press will go ape shit. He's our perfect candidate. I must have his footage," Fletcher said calmly.

The two men sat in silence, back to back, at an impasse.

"Is this about Laura?" Alan asked after a moment.

Fletcher's reaction was unexpectedly violent. "Don't even say her name! You don't know anything about that!" He took a moment to regain his composure, clearly unhappy to have given so much away. When he spoke again, his voice was calm. "It's not about her. These implants distort personal history and therefore all history. I will not stand by while the past is rewritten for the sake of pleasant Rememories."

He paused and Alan could almost hear his anger regaining the upper hand. "Tell me something," Fletcher asked, "why is your name the first on the list for cutting scumbags and lowlifes?"

"I forgive the guilty long after they can be punished for their sins," Alan answered.

"I know what you do. *Why* do you do it?" Fletcher persisted.

Alan took a moment to think seriously about the question. "Do you know what a Sin Eater is?" he asked.

"Sin Eater?"

"Sin eating is an ancient tradition from the British Isles," Alan explained. "When someone died, a Sin Eater was brought in. These people were social outcasts, marginals. The body of the deceased was laid out with bread and salt on the chest and coins over the eyes. The Sin Eater would eat the bread and salt and take the coins as payment. By doing this, the Eater absorbed the sins of the dead, cleansing their souls and giving them safe passage into the next life."

"What about the Sin Eater?" Fletcher asked. "Bearing the burden of all those wrongs?"

Alan let the queries sink in. "Are you worried about my soul, Fletcher?"

Alan stood as a train rumbled into the station. Fletcher stood as well. They faced one another through the wire mesh.

"I *will* have Bannister," Fletcher told him.

Alan shrugged. "I can't give him to you."

When Alan started to walk away, Fletcher, suddenly enraged, reached through the metal fence and managed to grab hold of the cutter's shirt.

"Hey, don't turn your back on me! You see that man behind me?"

For the first time, Alan noticed the young man with the faint tattoo silently watching a few feet away.

"I don't want to bring him into this conversation. But I will if you leave me no other choice," Fletcher said in a low, intense voice.

Alan pulled his shirt free of Fletcher's hold. Simon was definitely scary. He looked crazy, capable of anything. But so did Fletcher. Suddenly all Alan wanted to do was get as far away as possible from the fanatics. Without another word, he disappeared into the crowd.

On the other side of the platform, Fletcher held Simon back from climbing over the fence and going after Alan. It wasn't the time for violence.

Soon. But not yet.

TWELVE

Back at Alan's empty apartment, the Guillotine continued its assigned task, scrolling at nearly lightning speed, attempting to match the frozen face of Louis on the monitor with any other possible encounters between Charles Bannister and this single character: thousands and thousands of hours to search, a job only a computer might attempt.

While the search was in progress, Alan made his way into a smoky bar in a commercial section of town. It was afternoon and the patrons, almost entirely men, were badly dressed, bent over their drinks at tables and stools. There was no merriment in this place, only defeat. The air was thick with a haze of tobacco and the smell of stale beer.

Alan spotted a spidery middle-aged man in a rumpled suit. That fellow, who bore a striking resemblance to some subterranean creature who'd never seen the light of day, might well have spent his entire life in bars. The man nodded briefly, then carried a duffel bag into the bathroom at the back of the bar.

Alan followed and was almost overcome by the pungent odors in the bathroom. On the wall a condom dispenser bore photographs of lascivious women. The spidery man locked the door behind them.

"Where do I know you from again?" the predator asked. His eyes were red and mean, filled with low cunning and endless suspicion.

"You don't know me," Alan answered.

"Yeah, well, that ain't good enough, pal."

"A friend of mine recommended you. Billy Finch."

That name brought fear to the spidery man's face. One of the advantages of being a cutter was the ability to uncover unspeakable indiscretions others would rather keep hidden.

"B-B-B-Billy *who*?" the man demanded.

"Don't play games with me. I know you

too well for that. I know all your secrets. Oliver."

The mean red eyes opened wide in disbelief. "How do you know my name?"

"I know about the kittens you suffocated when you were thirteen. I know about the scar on your back." Alan stepped closer, menacingly. "You sold Billy Finch the gun he killed his brother with. You helped him bury the body."

As predators go, Oliver was not particularly dangerous, just a bottom feeder in the murky ocean of crime. He stared at Alan with terror in his eyes, baffled at how the stranger could know so much. He backed away as far as he could get until he was against the wall. His feet slipped and he slid down into the urinal. Oliver's collapse might have been comical under different circumstances.

"Yeah . . . yeah. So what?" Oliver managed, affecting a last show of bravado. "You're a cop?"

"No. Far from it. I want what Billy wanted: a gun." Alan took a roll of bills from his trousers and stuffed them in Oliver's breast pocket.

Sputtering with confusion, Oliver unzipped the duffel bag near his feet and pulled a revolver from it.

"Here. Take it," he said. "Take it and go."

Alan reached into the duffel bag and pulled out a small box of bullets. He knew everything about Oliver's business, even where the spidery man kept his ammunition. But he had never held a gun before. The weapon felt strange and heavy in his hands. Quickly, he examined the gun, then hid it inside his coat.

"Take care, Ollie," he said. "Be good."

Alan unlocked the door and left the bathroom, leaving Oliver squatting in the urinal, shuddering with fear.

The Chop Block rested on one of the tables near the deserted refreshment counter in the October Theater lobby. The monitor was alive with a Zoe film in progress. But this Zoe film was different from any Hasan had ever seen. It was in black and white and the point of view was odd, bouncing along low to the ground. In fact, it was from an experimental implant in a dog. On the screen, the dog stopped, turned, and began gnawing at its own fur. There was heavy panting on the soundtrack.

Thelma was in a black dress with a black hat, which had a white ribbon on it—a formal outfit appropriate for a Rememory she was about to attend. Michael was also dressed for a public occasion in a scruffy suit that looked as though it had come from a thrift shop. His black eye was faded purple.

"I can't take this," Hasan said finally.

With a shrug, Thelma shut down the Chop Block, putting an end to the show.

"Zoe Pet, they're calling it? Unbelievable!" Hasan said. "Who's gonna buy this shit?"

"The ancient Egyptians had their pets mummified with them. Not much different than this."

After Hasan left, Thelma put out her cigarette and gathered her equipment to leave. She and Michael were on their way to a doggie Rememory and had only stopped off long enough to show Hasan their work.

"Do you have the directions?" she asked Michael.

"Yes, yes, it's at the Whitechapel Theater,"

he told her curtly. "Been there a dozen times."

Thelma stood from the table to find Fletcher watching them silently from the doorway. "Well, hello, John."

Michael came up behind her. "Who are you?" he demanded.

"He's someone I used to know," Thelma explained, without taking her eyes off Fletcher. "You go on. I'll catch up in a minute."

Michael left the theater lobby grudgingly, taking Thelma's Chop Block with him. He hated to miss anything that might be interesting or useful to advance his career. When they were alone, Fletcher worked a smile onto his face.

"Hello, Thelma," he said. "You're looking beautiful as ever."

"Please, John. Stop yanking my chain. I haven't slept in three days. I look bulldozed."

His expression softened. "You were always the only one who called me John."

"If you're looking for Alan, he's not here," she said, unwilling to play the nostalgia game.

A moment of understanding seemed to pass between them; they had always seen through each other very well. Fletcher shrugged. "Alan isn't being reasonable," he said. "Talk to him, Thelma. He'll listen to you. Otherwise . . . he might get hurt. Bannister isn't worth protecting."

Thelma didn't answer immediately. "I don't despise your cause, John," she said carefully. "I understand it. I just despise your methods."

"You're in no position to talk ethics with me, Thelma. You passed on Bannister because you were too weak to watch. Your hands are as dirty as the next cutter."

"Maybe." Preparing to leave, Thelma put on dark glasses. "I'd love to stay and chat, but you'll have to excuse me. I have a Rememory to attend."

"It's gone too far," Fletcher called after her. "We've become a society of reflections."

But Thelma was already in motion, walking out the door to where Michael was waiting with the doggie Rememory in the Chop Block.

Thelma wondered vaguely what Fletcher would think of a canine Zoe, whether his scruples extended to the animal kingdom or only to humans. Probably the very idea of Zoe Pets would present all sorts of new moral issues for him to wrestle with. But she didn't have time to find out. With a whistle, Michael stopped a taxi and they sped away to deliver the final cut to the bereaved family waiting for it.

THIRTEEN

Alan arrived at the Bannister mansion late in the afternoon to find a dozen luxury cars parked in the driveway. He made his way past a handful of chauffeurs waiting beside their cars, smoking cigarettes, and making small talk.

Inside the white living room, the blinds were drawn, the lights dimmed. The room was filled with the extended Bannister family—old people, children, parents, and toddlers crowded together on the couch, on chairs, and on the floor. There was a buzz of the friendly banter of people who know one another well. They were getting set to watch a special showing on a giant screen that took up an entire wall of the room.

Alan was shown by a maid to the kitchen, which was huge and sterile and fitted with every cooking gadget known to man. Alan drank a cup of coffee at the table while he waited for Jennifer Bannister to make herself available. She came in after a few minutes, closing the door behind her. She was dressed elegantly in black. Everything about her was cold, beautiful, and glamorous. But she didn't appear happy to see him.

"I'm sorry to keep you, Mr. Hakman," she said, joining him at the table. "As you can see, this is a bad time. It's our tradition to screen the family tree the week before a Rememory. How is my husband coming along?"

"Well." Alan put down his coffee cup and studied her. "It's just so much material, and so little time. I was hoping you could give me some illumination."

"Okay. As much as I can."

She was barely polite, clearly anxious to get back to her living room full of family. Nevertheless, Alan took his time, flipping through blank pages of his notebook as though he were looking to understand key moments of Charles Bannister's life—a life he already understood far too well.

"Do you remember the moment you fell in love with your husband?" he asked after a moment.

"Oh, goodness . . . how can you answer a question like that?" She seemed put off. She obviously had to force herself even to think about it, reminding herself that it was essential to have a good Rememory film for her husband. To her, Alan was only a servant, like her maid or Filipino butler, but at the moment, he was a necessary servant. "Maybe . . . when he took me down to the pier, on the Fourth of July," she said finally, trying to breathe some life into the memory. "We were walking, and he was going on and on about—"

"This is during college?"

"Yes. I looked up at him and thought, 'This is the man I want to spend my life with.'"

Mrs. Bannister seemed eager to say the expected thing. In fact, Alan doubted she was the sort of woman who ever fell in love. Most likely it had been clear to her from the start that Charles Bannister was destined to become rich and powerful—reason enough for a woman like her to marry. As it happened, Alan couldn't care less about her love life. He cleared his throat and came to the real reason he was here today.

"I have a question about a man at one of your parties," he said, looking up from his notebook.

She cocked an eyebrow, surprised. "What man?"

"At a party from a year ago. He wore very thick glasses. He must have been—"

"Thick *glasses*?" she interrupted, clearly annoyed. "Mr. Hakman, how is this relevant? Minor people that I don't even know have no place in the Rememory. Family. Career. Community. That's all I want. Cut everything else."

Alan saw he wasn't going to get anywhere with this line of questioning. He closed his notebook. "I would like to talk with Isabel," he said.

Mrs. Bannister tensed visibly. "Right now?"

"It would be helpful."

Alan watched her inner struggle. For a moment, he thought she might simply ask him to leave. But then she seemed to decide that it was better under the circumstances to cooperate.

"Yes, of course," she said brightly. "I'll go let her know."

Alan waited in Isabel's bedroom, sitting on her bed, while her mother went to find the child. The huge room overflowed with stuffed animals. Bright with sunlight and colorful wallpaper, it was the ultimate little girl's room, perfect in every detail, yet somehow dead. It was hard to imagine how a real child could live there. Alan picked up a toy bear lying facedown on the pillow and rearranged it so that the bear was sitting up.

The door opened and Isabel, led by her mother, walked in. She was pretty, but she didn't look happy.

"Now do as I told you," her mother said in a false singsongy voice. "Mr. Hakman wants to talk to you about Daddy. It's for Daddy's movie."

Deliberately ignoring Alan, the little girl went directly to a corner of her room and began playing with a dollhouse. Mrs. Bannister looked at Alan with a mixture of apprehension and regret.

Then someone called from the next room,

"Jennifer? Are you coming back? We're starting."

The mother paused anxiously. It was obvious that she knew what her husband had been doing to their daughter. For a moment, Alan thought she was going to say something, perhaps by way of explanation or apology. But in the end, she turned and left the room without a word, closing the door behind her.

Alan turned his attention to the little girl who was still playing with her dollhouse. "Hello, Isabel. My name is Alan."

Isabel didn't answer. She was busy leading two of her dolls into the dollhouse. Alan opened the door, sensing that, with her history, doing so might make the child more comfortable.

"What's going on in there?" he asked, standing next to her dollhouse while she played. He felt very much like a huge, awkward adult.

"A birthday party for the frog man," Isabel answered.

"Oh. That's nice." Alan glanced around the room, then sat back on the bed. "Isabel, could you come sit with me a minute?"

"Okay."

She sat on the very end of the bed, holding a doll protectively in her arms. She kept her head down and kicked her legs obsessively back and forth.

"Who's that?" Alan asked in his most comforting voice.

"My doll."

"What's her name?"

"She doesn't have a name. She's just a doll." Isabel shook the doll by the hair, to show him that it had no feelings at all. "See?"

"Isabel, your father—"

"My daddy is the best daddy in the world," she told him quickly. "He had a really big meeting one day, but instead he took me horseback riding."

Alan tried to think of a way to approach the subject he had in mind. "I—"

But she interrupted again. "He would read me stories before bed every night. Sometimes he would make them up as he went, and I knew but I didn't care."

Alan studied the little girl's face as she talked. Everything she said seemed rehearsed and stilted. Meanwhile, she never raised her head. She kept her eyes on her feet, which she continued to kick back and forth.

Alan saw he needed to change his approach. "Your mom said I'm here to talk to you about your dad. But we don't have to if you don't want," he said.

"I don't want to," Isabel told him sullenly.

"Then we won't."

They sat together for a while in a companionable silence. "I was only a few years older than you when I lost both my parents," Alan said. He glanced at her to see if he was getting through, but there was no response from her at all. Nothing. He sighed. "You don't want me here, nosing around, asking questions. And you're right."

Isabel looked up at him for the first time, her guard down.

"Not many people know what you are feeling. Not many people understand," he said. "But I do."

"Okay," she told him.

They sat for another few moments in silence.

"Alan?"

"Yes?"

"Today isn't really the frog man's birthday. It's next week."

He smiled at her and she giggled.

"I have one question, and then I'm gone," he said. "I'm looking for a man who was at a party your parents had. He wore glasses, thick as a glass bottle."

"Mr. Hunt," she replied without hesitation. "I took him the invitation."

"Mr. Hunt . . . Louis Hunt?"

"He was my teacher."

Alan could barely contain his excitement. "What does he teach?"

She shook her head. "He doesn't teach anymore. He died in a car accident. It was really sad. We had a remembrance day for him at school."

"A Rememory? He had a Rememory?"

But again the little girl shook her head. "No. Just a day at school when we talked about him."

Alan stood up from her bed. "Thank you, Isabel," he said gratefully.

He began to leave, but she stopped him.

"Alan?"

He turned back to her.

"Are you going to fix what Daddy can remember?" she asked.

"In a way. Yes."

She hesitated, looking away. "Please make

him forget the time I drew on his contracts with crayon."

"I will."

"And the time I pulled Dotty's hair so hard she cried. Will he forget that?"

Alan looked into the little girl's eyes and felt a strange kinship with her.

"He'll forget," he told her solemnly. "But make sure you don't."

FOURTEEN

Alan had the same nightmare again and again. The images were disoriented, drunken. This is what he dreamed:

A child opens his hand and stares at the ivory talisman on a leather hoop, a tangible memento of horror. The talisman itself is frightening, ominous. . . .

And now, with the crazy logic of dreams, the child is running down the concrete stairs in the half-finished building, wanting only to get away, tears streaming down his face.

The boy leaps down the steps, crashing on the landings, turning corners, one after another. Then suddenly he stops. There on the wall where he scrawled it earlier, the letters of his name blaze back at him.

The sight stabs at him, piercing, judging, accusing. You can get away from almost anything, even an unfinished building in the nightmare of your memories. But you can never get away from yourself. . . .

There was music playing in Hasan's workshop when the phone began to ring. Hasan was underneath his Guillotine with tools in hand. He might have been a mechanic working on a car. The Guillotine was more complicated than any motorized vehicle, but Hasan had the editing console almost completely disassembled, with various pieces lying on the floor around him. Unlike Alan, Hasan enjoyed getting into the nuts and bolts of the machine.

Whistling to the music, Hasan slid out from under the Guillotine and did his best to ignore the telephone. But it kept ringing insistently.

"Fine, fine," he said with irritation; then he answered the call. "Hello?"

It was Alan. And Alan wanted a favor—a difficult favor, as it turned out. But of course, Alan was a difficult man.

*   *   *

Later that night, Hasan drove through the city in his pickup truck. Alan sat beside him, staring nervously at the rearview mirror from time to time to see if they were being followed. Unfortunately, at night in city traffic, with a profusion of lights coming from many directions, he couldn't be sure one way or the other.

Meanwhile, Hasan was enjoying himself. In fact, there was seldom a moment when Hasan didn't enjoy himself. He glanced over to the passenger seat and smirked.

"Would you relax, Alan? There's nobody following us."

Realizing Hasan was right, Alan relaxed a little.

"This is a pretty big favor I'm doing for you," Hasan said grandly. "You're just lucky my cousin Karim is working late tonight."

They continued to drive in silence through the city. Alan could sit for long periods without saying a word, but Hasan preferred talk. He was garrulous; silence was one of the few things that made him uncomfortable.

"So . . . how are things with you and Delila?" he asked.

"Delila?" Alan sighed. "I think I've messed that up for good."

"Do you want her?"

"Yes. I *need* her."

"Does she want you?" Hasan asked pointedly.

"I think so. Sometimes. But . . ."

"But what?"

"You tell me."

"I don't know this woman, but may I speak frankly?"

Alan nodded.

"Man, you're a prick! Chill out. Stop by the side of the road and sit under an apple tree. You know what I mean?"

Alan considered Hasan's words. His impulse was to become defensive, but he saw the truth in what Hasan had said. He nodded again.

They came to a converted brownstone building on a quiet street. An expensive sign above the front door read EYE TECH ADMINISTRATIVE. Hasan parked a few doors down from the building. He locked his pickup and led the way along a narrow walkway to the rear of the brownstone until they came to a metal door with no handle. Almost immediately, the door opened from the inside with a clang. Hasan checked around them, then ducked inside the building with Alan close behind him. They made their way together through the narrow corridors of the building until they came to a hallway, where Hasan's cousin Karim was waiting. Karim was a thin young man with sad eyes. He was dressed in the official Eye Tech uniform, with the company logo on the sleeve.

"I could lose my job letting cutters in here," he said nervously.

"Come now, Karim, would I get you in trouble?" Hasan replied in his grand manner.

Less than reassured by his cousin's nonchalance, Karim led them through the building to a darkened file room. After he unlocked the door, Alan and Hasan flicked on their flashlights.

"They can track anyone accessing data through a computer. This is the best I can do. Please hurry." Karim glanced anxiously up and down the corridor outside, then locked all three of them inside.

Alan set to work with frantic speed. He walked up and down the aisles looking for the letter H on the file cabinets. It would have been much better to have access to the computers, but since that was impossible, the old-fashioned method would have to do: hard copies of customer files, each in a separate manila folder.

"Calm down," Hasan said. "If this guy had a Zoe Implant, there will be a record of it here."

"Louis Hunt," Alan muttered, going through the alphabetical listings. "Hunt . . . Louis Hunt . . ."

As Alan searched, Hasan grabbed a file at random from the shelf. Inside, he found various legal documents and a small disk in a sleeve.

"What the hell is this little thing?" Hasan asked, holding up the disk.

"That's the Zoe Family Greeting," Karim said. "It comes with the premium packages . . . so naturally you've never seen one."

"What's that supposed to mean?"

Alan tuned out the voices of the two other men, who began bickering in Arabic. He was sweating heavily in the dusty room, pointing his flashlight at the H section, working his way through the files.

"Shhh!" Karim whispered suddenly. "Someone's coming!"

Immediately, Hasan and Alan switched off their flashlights. They waited in the dark as footsteps approached the door to the file room. The shadow of two feet appeared at the crack beneath the door. Alan closed his eyes and held his breath, unable to bear the tension. The knob turned, but whoever was checking the door found it locked. Then came the sound of someone walking away down the corridor.

"Hurry up!" Karim whispered urgently once the intruder was gone. "Either it's here or it isn't!"

Alan resumed his search, hunting alphabetically through the H section. He scanned past Hullings, Hunnicut, Hunziker, but no Louis Hunt. Carefully, he thumbed through the files again to make certain he hadn't missed it, but no Louis Hunt. Apparently, he didn't have a Zoe Implant.

Alan dropped his head and clenched his fists in disappointment. He was about to turn away when something caught his eye: Horowitz . . . Hennesey . . . Hamendale . . .

Hakman. With trembling fingers, he pulled out his own file.

Terrified, Alan glanced behind him. Hasan and Karim waited impatiently near the door, still chatting in Arabic. Luckily, they weren't paying attention to him. Quickly, Alan slipped the file under his coat.

"Any luck?" Hasan asked.

"No . . . no luck," Alan answered. "No record of him having a chip."

"Well, that's that."

Karim was glad to see them go. Alan felt sick to his stomach as he rode away from the Eye Tech Administration building in the passenger seat of Hasan's truck. A sheen of cold sweat appeared on his forehead.

He had broken the first rule of his profession. He knew it was forbidden for a cutter to have a Zoe Implant. The indiscretion was overwhelming. If anyone discovered his secret, he would never be allowed to work again.

"You look like you're getting sick," Hasan said. "Fever."

"I'm fine," Alan managed.

The truck pulled over near Alan's apartment.

"Thanks, Hasan." Alan fumbled with the door handle and stood up unsteadily from the cab.

"See you at the October," Hasan said, a strange expression playing over his face.

Alan was relieved to be alone. With a dizzy sense of anticipation, he hurried upstairs to look at his file.

FIFTEEN

As soon as he was upstairs, Alan carried the
stolen file to his Guillotine, deeply unsettled at
the prospect of seeing his own Zoe documents.
On the big monitor, the track of Bannister's Zoe
continued to run, but that matter suddenly
held little importance. Taking a deep breath,
Alan opened the envelope with unsteady fingers. A disk slipped out of its sleeve and fell
onto the floor. Alan stared at it a moment, then
bent over to pick it up. Printed on its front
were the simple yet terrifying words:

WELCOME TO THE ZOE FAMILY!

Alan fumbled the disk into the main drive,
then pressed the PLAY button. The Eye Tech

logo appeared and the company's signature music blared out. Then came a shot of a well-dressed, amicable man sitting behind an oak desk in a well-appointed office. The man addressed the camera directly.

"Hello, Mr. and Mrs. Hakman, and welcome to the Zoe family. You have made an important decision, a decision that will affect your lineage for generations to come. You have purchased a Zoe Implant for your unborn son. What does this mean? Immortality. Your son's life will live on forever, to be enjoyed by his great-great-grandchildren a century from now. No longer do our most cherished moments together have to fade and disappear over time."

From a different angle, the smooth-talking Eye Tech representative continued his presentation. Everything about him and his office suggested respectability and prosperity.

"Remember, the Zoe Implant is entirely organic. Since it grows with your baby's brain and nerve centers, it is virtually undetectable. When is the right time to tell your child about this miraculous gift? Well, that varies from person to person. Our studies indicate that by their twenty-first birthday, most carriers are mature enough to understand. From then on, your son can live his life and know that always and forever, his experiences and adventures will be revisited and relished. And *that's* what great memories are made of!"

As the screen faded to black, Alan let out his breath and struggled to inhale. Watching the contents of the disk was excruciating. After a moment white words appeared over the black background:

Initialization. Supervising Surgeon:
Emily Williams

The blackness faded and revealed a new scene: a hospital room. Alan's mother lay on a bed, about six months pregnant. She was connected to a high-tech assortment of tubes, wires, and digital screens. Alan's father stood beside her, holding her hand. A nurse waited nearby.

The woman doctor displayed an electronic syringe up for the camera to see. Inside the syringe were a green liquid and many tiny carbon colored strands: the organic stew that made up the Zoe Implant.

"Don't be alarmed," the doctor said in a

comforting voice. "This is as safe as procedures get."

"Is it necessary to film it?" Alan's mother asked. Her voice quavered, not entirely steady, revealing her anxiety.

"It's good to have, Mrs. Hakman," the doctor said with a patronizing smile. "Some cutters like to use it in the Rememory. It has a certain dramatic power."

The doctor approached Mrs. Hakman with the syringe. One monitor showed her womb. Shyly, Mrs. Hakman lifted her gown, exposing her pregnant belly. The doctor brought the needle close, until it was touching her stomach.

Alan couldn't bear to watch the images of himself inside his mother's womb about to receive the implant. In a single violent motion, he yanked the disk from the drive and hurled it across the room, where it hit the wall and shattered.

For nearly all his adult life, Alan had been dealing with Zoe Implants in other people's lives, but he had never imagined what it would be like to have one himself. He stormed into his bathroom and stared into the mirror, opening his eyes wide. He couldn't see it, but he knew it was there inside him . . .

recording this moment forever! The thought was terrible, and for a moment, Alan felt he was going crazy.

He let out a strangled yelp. He punched out at the mirror in fury and despair, cracking the glass, fracturing his reflection.

Somewhere in his brain, the Zoe Implant was recording his agony and marking it with his exact age:

A. HAKMAN: 51 YEARS: 183 DAYS:
23 HOURS

Alan couldn't sleep, couldn't think, couldn't bear living within his own skin. The next day, unable to remain in his apartment, he went out on the street to try to get away. Unfortunately, he couldn't escape from the Zoe Implant. He staggered like a drunk man down a crowded sidewalk.

It was astonishing how his discovery had changed his perception of reality. He passed a billboard on a nearby building:

Eye Tech
Life in All Its Glory!

Although Alan had seen this billboard for months, he had never before longed to howl with laughter at it. Glory? No, it was madness!

He stared into the eyes of other pedestrians. No one could meet his gaze for long, of course. Finally he chanced upon a balding man with a familiar face, though he couldn't quite place him.

"You! I know you!" he cried, grabbing the man by the shoulders.

"Get your hands off me!" The man slapped Alan away.

"I know you. . . ."

The man fled. Alan knew he was making a spectacle of himself, but he couldn't stop. He spun around and glared at the crowd gathering around him.

"I know all of you!" he screamed. He lurched in circles, trying to make the others vanish. At last he crumpled to the ground, his head in his hands.

"You make me sick," he said softly. He lay on the sidewalk in an exhausted heap.

The people walked away, muttering insults: "Weirdo . . . drunk . . ."

Alan kept still. How would that scene play

out on a cutter's monitor? With a sigh, he turned on his back and stared up at the billboard above him:

Eye Tech
Life in All Its Glory!

"Alan?" Delila crouched beside him, blocking out the billboard. She reached for his arm. "Can you stand? You're feverish."

Gratefully, he allowed Delila to pull him to his feet and lead him home.

SIXTEEN

Later that night, Alan sat on his bed with his shirt and jacket off. He didn't entirely remember how he had gotten home or how the rest of the day had passed. He was exhausted. Delila was there with him—that was the important thing. She stood next to the bed, pressing a wet cloth on his forehead.

"What happened to you?" she asked, but Alan was unable to answer.

The Guillotine was still running the track on Louis. With a spurt of anger, Delila grabbed Alan's shirt and draped it over the monitor. "You can't let your work get to you like this."

Alan put his hand over hers. "Don't leave."

She studied him, undecided. "The bookstore's closed tomorrow," she said quietly after a moment. "I don't have to go."

It wasn't exactly a long-term commitment, but Alan was grateful for every second he was able to keep Delila from walking out the door. He was starting to feel better. He stood on unsteady legs. For a second, dizziness swept over him. When the vertigo passed, he sat in the editing chair.

"What've you got to eat in this dump?" Delila asked.

She opened the fridge: a dozen eggs, a bottle of soda water, a lone olive floating in rank liquid. She tried the cupboards: three cans of soup, some exotic nuts, packets of ketchup, mustard, and soy sauce. Delila held up the nuts, which were in a package with Chinese characters.

"I saw them in a project." He shrugged. "They looked good."

Delila opened the package and popped a nut in her mouth. She gagged and spat it out. "Yuck. They're disgusting. And they look like little rabbit turds. I think they *are* rabbit turds. I guess we order out then." She dropped the offending nuts in the trash.

Delila sat on the bed watching him. Alan

looked back into her eyes and felt all her living warmth. After a moment, he produced a small key from his pocket and unlocked the bottom drawer on his Guillotine. Inside the drawer were a half dozen disks. He searched until he found the one he was after.

"No," Delila told him firmly. "I don't want to see any more."

"These are different." He loaded the disk into the Guillotine. Immediately, a Zoe montage began to show on the largest monitor, and it was different from the usual Zoe sequences. Not every image was a point-of-view shot. Some actually showed the subject.

In the first scene, a man sat behind the wheel of a car parked in a garage. Slowly, a school of tropical fish began swimming by outside the windshield. It was weird, yet somehow wonderful.

There was a dissolve to a flock of sheep grazing on the asphalt acres of a used-car lot, a startling juxtaposition between rural and urban.

"What is this?" Delila asked with a smile.

Alan gestured for her just to watch a new scene. Someone was being pushed on a swing, sailing back and forth. The motion was soothing. Back and forth, up and down, a wild ride . . . but then the swing appeared to break loose of its moorings and gravity as well. It soared high into the sky through the soft dreamy air, with the world rushing by below. Delila laughed with delight.

"Certain implant models have a defect," Alan explained. "They can't tell the difference between what you see and what you think you see."

"So what are these? Dreams?"

"Dreams. Daydreams. Nightmares. Hallucinations."

The montage of defective Zoe images continued. Next, a dog trotted through an empty street, gingerly carrying a stuffed toy dog in its teeth. The images dissolved to a pretty girl in a thin white dress. She was dancing seductively in front of a young man hypnotized by the very sight of her. But every time he reached out to touch her, he found her just out of reach.

The monitor went black as the montage came to an end. Delila turned to Alan with renewed affection. The images he had showed her *were* wonderful. She could understand the beauty he found in them. But she could see also that Alan was far from well. As she watched, he coughed violently and nearly collapsed. Gently, she led him from the editing console to his bed, helped him get off his clothes, and tucked him under the covers.

When he was in bed, she lay down beside him, snuggling close. "Every time I think I've had it with you, you show me something amazing," she said softly.

Alan wasn't certain how long he slept. When he woke it was night and his head was clear. He knew exactly what he had to do. All the lights were off in the apartment and Delila was asleep beside him on the bed, fully dressed. Her breathing was regular, tickling his neck very slightly as she inhaled and exhaled.

He got up carefully so as not to wake her and gazed down at her sleeping form while he put on his clothes. He loved Delila more than he had loved anything or anyone in his entire life. But he needed to rid himself of the Zoe Implant embedded in his brain before he could be with her. Without a word, Alan left the apartment, closing the door behind him silently so as not to disturb her.

SEVENTEEN

Fletcher was sitting in his car at the curb with Simon, the young fanatic with tattoos, when Alan came walking out the front door of his building. Fletcher and Simon watched through the windshield as Alan glanced about nervously up and down the street, then slipped off down an alley. His stealthy movements were suspicious. But for all his caution, Alan had not noticed the two men watching him.

"Where are you off to, Alan?" Fletcher wondered quietly to himself.

"That's him?" Simon asked, sitting up suddenly and paying attention.

"Yeah."

Simon glanced up at Alan's window, dark

and blank above the street, then started to open the car door.

"Not now," Fletcher told him. "There's somebody up there. This has to be clean. No mess."

Reluctantly, Simon closed the car door and remained in the passenger seat.

"Clean. Dirty. All the same to me," he said. "We'll come back."

Without a word in reply, Fletcher started the car and drove off. But this wasn't finished. As Simon said, they would be back.

Alan's destination was an old part of town, a colorful neighborhood with streets lined with small music clubs and cafés, head shops and used-record stores where you could find old vinyl editions from long-forgotten bands. It was the part of the city where hip young people, as well as prostitutes and drug dealers and hustlers of every kind, liked to go.

Alan stood across the street from a tattoo parlor with a garishly painted sign: LOUP GAROU. Punk music blasted from the open door, and in the window were tattoo samples in every imaginable shape and color. Near the door lounged slackers with shaved heads, tattooed skin, pierced nostrils, and tight black clothing.

Alan's nerves were ragged. The tattoo parlor reeked of danger, chaos. As a cutter, he had spent his life organizing random moments into a coherent whole. These people, he sensed, tore apart whatever they came in contact with.

He glanced at the red flyer, with its bold print, in his hand to make certain this was the right place:

SYNTH TATTOOS
OUR WAY OF FIGHTING BACK

Overcoming his revulsion, he walked across the street and in the door. His neat appearance made him stand out. Several of the multitattooed punks sneered at him suspiciously, but they grudgingly gave way. Alan trembled slightly at the counter until a muscular man in a sleeveless T-shirt noticed him. Awkwardly, Alan did his best to explain what he wanted, but for all his efforts, he might have been speaking a different language. The man motioned for Alan to come closer.

"You see Legz over there?" the man whispered. He pointed behind the counter to where a woman in her thirties with a hard, sexy face lounged. "You need to follow her."

The woman headed down a flight of narrow stairs into the basement room below. The room was dark, crowded, and musty. Only one small window let in a meager shaft of streetlight. In the center of the room, a reclining chair was surrounded by the tools of the tattoo trade: needles and dyes. The stale smell of sweat and cigarette smoke hung in the air. Every muscle in Alan's body wanted to turn and bolt. But he forced himself forward and sat in the chair.

"What design do you want?" Legz asked.

Alan forced his eyes her way. Legz was not a pleasant sight, with all the piercings in her nose, her eyebrows, her ears, and even her exposed navel.

"Are you qualified to do this?" Alan asked.

Legz smiled unpleasantly. "I have a PhD in neurosurgery, okay? I just enjoy drawing on skin a hell of a lot more than cutting into it."

He watched apprehensively as she pulled up a chair and switched on a lamp.

"Now you understand how this works?" she asked.

"No."

"We draw synth tattoos with electrosyn-
thetic ink. It creates a magnetic field that in-
terferes with the Zoe Implant, blocking it
from recording audio or video from that
point on."

She grabbed hold of an elaborate tattoo needle and brought it close to Alan's face. He
blinked and fought a wild urge to leap from
the chair. He had no alternative.

"First we do the audio tattoo. We wait a
week," she went on. "If you don't get mi-
graines and your system takes it, we do the
video tattoo."

Alan clutched the arms of his chair. "Does
it . . . does it need to cover my whole face?"

"No. Those guys are just young and angry.
You want it discreet?"

Alan nodded. "Very discreet."

Without another word, Legz set to work.
She was professional in her own way—Alan
had to give her that. Nevertheless, he winced
as the needle pierced his skin.

Several hours later, Alan walked back to his
apartment. He climbed the stairs slowly, exhausted from little sleep. His face hurt and

his legs were weak from tension. He took out his keys and was about to unlock his front door when he heard a strange muffled noise coming from inside his apartment. He pressed his ear against the door. It sounded like someone was at his Guillotine.

He tensed. His mouth was suddenly dry with fear. He took the gun from his left pocket, and from the other pocket, he pulled the small box of bullets. Concentrating to keep his hand from shaking, he loaded the gun. Then he snapped the chamber shut quietly. At last, he used his key to open the door.

"Fletcher?" he called. "I'm armed. I have a gun."

There was no response. Carefully, he walked inside with the gun pointing the way. There was a figure seated at his Guillotine, but it wasn't Fletcher. To his surprise, Delila seated at the editing console. She turned when she heard him. There were tears welling in her eyes. Alan lowered the gun and looked about, trying to understand what the problem could be.

The bottom drawer of the Guillotine was open with the tiny key still in the lock from the night before. Several disks were scattered on the Guillotine. On the monitors, the track of Charles Bannister continued to scroll, moment after moment of the attorney's life. But on the largest monitor, a very different lifetime was playing, the final cut of an old Zoe project. Alan felt like someone had just kicked him in the stomach. He understood suddenly why Delila was upset, and horrible despair filled him.

The large monitor showed the Zoe Rememories of Delila's old boyfriend. The first shot showed Delila falling over and laughing as she learned to ski on a mountain of fluffy white snow. Then the scene shifted and she was kissing her old boyfriend's face, her eyes glittering with love. Then, in another scene, Delila was getting dressed up for a party, fumbling with her shoes. And finally, Delila was naked on a bed in a passionate embrace, her face against that of her onetime lover.

Alan set the gun down on the table and struggled to find the right words. But he was tongue-tied; he had no excuse. Delila held back tears as the montage continued to play behind her.

"Not so hard to make this thing play disks," she said in an unnatural voice. "Not hard at all."

"Delila—"

"Shut up! This is my old boyfriend, you bastard. I . . . is *this* why you wanted to be with me? You saw . . . you saw some proof that I'm to your liking?"

She swallowed hard, struggling with her feelings. Then she pointed angrily at the monitor. "These moments belong to *me*, Alan! They're mine. And his. Who are you to take them away from me?"

It was too much for her. She burst into tears of rage and hurt, then charged at Alan, her hands clawing, punching, and shoving. Alan tried to restrain her, but she was out of control. With an animal growl, she scratched him across the face, just missing his eye. The gash filled with blood. He held his face, coughing from the pain, when Delila grabbed the gun from the table and aimed it at the Guillotine.

"No!" Alan cried. He saw what she was about to do only at the last moment. The gun fired with a loud explosion. There was a sickening crash of glass and metal as the bullet ripped through the computer. A spark flared from the console as all the monitors came to life, filled with a hundred lifetimes racing across the screens, warping and quivering. The speakers screamed in a multitude of voices and sounds. And then the monitors went black.

Delila dropped the gun. "Why am I so surprised?" Her voice seethed with fury. She jabbed at the disk drive until it opened, then jerked out the unlabeled disk, snapped it in two, and threw the pieces on the floor.

"Mine," she said. She was finished. Without another word, she left his apartment, slamming the door behind him.

Alone, Alan stood before the wreckage of his editing equipment. For several seconds he couldn't move. Finally, he reached out to the Guillotine, but it sparked again dangerously and he was forced to pull back his hand. Carefully, he tried a second time. He reached through the crackling electricity and pulled out the primary drive. But it was useless. He saw immediately that the bullet had gone right through it. The disk with the Bannister master was completely destroyed.

For Alan, it was hard to absorb all these disasters at once: Delila's rage, the destruction of his editing console, the loss of Bannister's disk. He turned toward the devastation and saw, to his astonishment, that one of the monitors was still alive with the frozen image of Louis Hunt burned onto the screen: Louis as an adult in his wheelchair, his thick eyeglasses propped up on his nose. Alan felt a wave of irrational fury rise up within him.

"I killed you, and it ruined my life!" he shouted at the screen. "How can you be there?"

But the frozen image on the monitor did not respond. It was crazy. Everything was gone. His life was in ruins. And still this mystery remained. How had Louis Hunt, the boy Alan believed he'd killed, grown up to become Isabel Bannister's teacher?

Suddenly, with a sharp sense of understanding, Alan reached to the synth tattoo, a pause symbol, on his neck. He almost laughed because the disaster was complete. Unwittingly, he had ruined his one chance to discover the truth.

Or had he? Was it too late?

EIGHTEEN

Hasan's workshop was a cramped space full of wires, electronic chips, motherboards, and all kinds of monitors in various states of repair. Hasan examined the primary drive from Alan's Guillotine. If anyone could repair the drive, Hasan was the man.

"Let me see." Hasan slipped on a pair of magnifying goggles. He turned on a bright reading light and spent several minutes poking at the primary drive with a pair of metal tweezers, his every grunt or frown raising or dashing Alan's hopes. Finally he sighed and shook his head.

"Alan, this thing is junked. The Zoe Implant itself is severed. God himself couldn't retrieve the footage. You know that."

Alan stared at the floor, disappointed but not surprised. He had known there was no hope. But the ruined implant wasn't entirely the reason he was here.

"We need to access a different life," Alan said.

"Well, where is it?" Hasan asked.

Slowly, Alan tapped his forehead with his finger.

Hasan stared at him, not understanding. "What? What are you talking about?"

"My implant, Hasan."

Hasan's eyes bulged wider than Alan had ever seen them before. *"What?"*

"The one in my head," Alan told him.

Hasan's surprise turned quickly to rage. "You snake! Never a word to any of us! Everything I've said to you, rattling around inside your skull!"

"Look," Alan said. "I can't—"

With a savage punch, Hasan smashed the other cutter's jaw. Alan collapsed on the floor, blessedly unconscious. It was the best thing that had happened to him in several hours.

Alan had no idea how long he'd been out. When he opened his eyes, he was still in Hasan's workshop and the window to the street showed him it was night. Hasan was standing above him, and next to Hasan, Thelma was seated on a chair.

Alan rubbed his jaw. His entire body seemed to ache in sharp pulses, but physical pain was the least of his worries at the moment.

"You want to take a shot at me, too?" he asked Thelma. "Everyone else has." He turned to Hasan. "I deserved that."

"You deserve more than that, Hakman," Hasan snarled. "I've half a mind to crack your ugly head open and pull the implant out with my teeth, along with anything else I find in there."

Thelma shook her head, like a disappointed mother. "Why didn't you tell us?"

"I didn't know until I found my records at Eye Tech," Alan explained. "I never thought my parents could afford one. It says they took out a loan to get it."

"How could you not know?" Hasan demanded.

"They died before they told me. Just . . . never got around to it."

"You know the Code, Alan," Thelma said.

"It's one of our central tenets. A cutter cannot have a Zoe Implant."

Alan looked from Thelma to Hasan. "I need to access my footage," he said quietly. "I need to do it now."

"That's impossible," Hasan told him curtly.

"No, it's possible. It's been done before. By you." When Hasan didn't reply, Alan continued. "Thelma told me about it: an attempt to retrieve footage from an implant while the carrier was still alive."

"I performed it," Hasan admitted unhappily, his voice flat. "The woman didn't recover. I won't try it again."

Alan studied Hasan, wondering how to convince him. "Then you know what it's like to be haunted," he said. "One memory, one single stinking accident has made me who I am. It won't leave me. The guilt is tearing up my mind. But now I have this chance to know the truth. And I have to take it."

Hasan's eyes were full of bitter accusation. "You brought an implant amongst us. Why should I help you?"

"Because I'll die for sure if I try it alone. And I *will* try it alone."

There was a pause as Alan let his words

sink in. Hasan rubbed his head and glanced at Thelma.

"We've been friends for years, Alan," Thelma said after a moment, weighing her words carefully. "I won't let you kill yourself. But a cutter with a Zoe Implant is a breach of the Code. You can never cut again."

Alan nodded his agreement, knowing this was as good a deal as he was ever going to get.

NINETEEN

An hour later, everything was ready. Alan sat patiently on a stool in the editing area of Hasan's workshop, waiting for his fate to reveal itself. Outside the window, the night seemed more silent and still, only an occasional siren far away. Soon, either he would know the secret of his childhood or his brain would be a burned-out circuit, beyond the cares of memory. He felt oddly at peace.

While Hasan was busy arranging his equipment, Thelma said to Alan, "Listen, the danger with what we are about to do—you still want to do this, right?"

When Alan nodded, she continued. "The danger is, we are going to reverse the Zoe Implant. When we make it transmit information instead of capturing it, it might transmit *to* your brain instead of *from* your brain."

"I understand."

"Do you, though? That means you'll have five decades of junk suddenly crashing into your cerebral cortex. Last time, the woman's nervous system couldn't handle it. It shut down immediately. Silence. She was a blank for the rest of her life."

Alan considered the effect of fifty-one years of memory crashing in upon him. Would his cerebral cortex overload as with the woman Hasan had tried to help? Well, it didn't matter. To be a blank the rest of his life wouldn't be any worse than what he was going through at that moment. It might even be an improvement.

Hasan indicated that he was ready. He had Alan move from the stool onto a nearby table. He picked up five small metal disks, each the size of a coin. They were attached by wires to Alan's laptop Chop Block. Hasan began to place them onto Alan's head. He attached two of the disks to Alan's temples, one beneath his chin and one at his crown. While he was attaching the final disk at the nape of Alan's neck, Hasan noticed the synth tattoo. Hasan shook his head, but made no comment.

Finally, Hasan sat down and faced Alan. He also had a laptop computer, his own Chop Block, which was connected to Alan's machine with a web of wires and cords.

"Remember, you can't copy anything to a drive," Hasan said. "You can only watch. Do you know where to look?"

"Yes."

"You have five minutes. After that, the risk's too high."

Hasan took a moment to bring up a digital timer on the screen of his computer. He set the counter to three hundred seconds.

"I hope I can see this coming. I don't want you on my conscience," Hasan said grumpily.

Alan nodded, indicating that he knew the dangers and wished to proceed. Despite his obvious misgivings, Hasan punched a series of commands into the computer and the metal disks attached to Alan's head began to vibrate gently. At first there was nothing. Then Alan's eyes opened wide, as though he had just received an electric shock. He gripped the table with both hands. On Hasan's screen, green waves began to fluctuate. Alan's screen came alive with a burst of static showing a profusion of unfixed patterns, colors and shapes.

At last, an image emerged from the chaos on Alan's screen: that very moment as Alan's eyes perceived it, with Hasan and Thelma standing in front of him. Alan scanned the room and the point-of-view image on the screen did the same. It was unnerving to see. He looked down at the monitor, where the screen showed an endless series of monitors within monitors.

Alan was as ready as he would ever be. He typed a series of commands on his keyboard and waited anxiously to see what would happen. The screen of Hasan's laptop continued to pulsate with green waves, but suddenly Alan's monitor showed something very different, a distant scene from his childhood. There he was, ten years old, 311 days, and fourteen hours, according to the readout in the lower right-hand corner of the screen. He was standing in the frozen-food section of a supermarket, kissing a girl. Alan was overwhelmed with emotion. It was his first love, a girl named Michelle, a neighbor from down the street. He had forgotten her existence until this moment, but at the age of ten she had been the most important thing in his life, a major obsession.

Michelle! It was unbelievable to see her again! Of course, she wasn't nearly as pretty as his memory of her, only a slightly chubby little girl with a mischievous face. But to re-live this moment, to stand in that super-market where he and Michelle had gone to buy Popsicles on a long-ago blazing summer day, and now to push his face forward until he touched her lips—for Alan, those things were nothing short of incredible.

He continued to watch in fascination as the scenes changed. He relived his parents' fu-neral, standing in a room surrounded by peo-ple dressed in black. All the adults were in tears. On the screen, Alan saw the open coffin, his father's face so strange in death, with the familiar cheeks slightly rouged from the mor-tician's brush. As Alan watched, a fly landed on his father's lip. Without thinking, young Alan reached out and brushed it away.

Then he was in his old childhood bedroom picking a scab on his knee. He peeled it off slowly and brought it up to his eyes. Dis-gusting! And yet there was something intriguing about the scab as well, at least from a boy's point of view. After a moment, he cautiously put the scab to his mouth and took an experimental taste.

"Blech!" said young Alan. With interest, the boy turned toward a mirror and inspected his tongue, looking at the scab resting on the tip. Looking down at the monitor from where he sat on the table, the adult Alan locked eyes with his childhood self. The two seemed to stare at one another across an abyss of time.

Meanwhile, on Hasan's screen, the fluctuations of the green waves increased. The timer read 179 seconds.

"Alan!" Hasan said in a warning voice.

Alan snapped out of his reverie. It was too easy to become seduced by the hypnotic images he saw on his screen. He felt like a visitor to a mysterious new planet; he wanted to linger in each of the fascinating moments passing by. But he needed to get to the event that concerned him, which meant jumping back at least a year in time. He hit a few keys on his keyboard; the images on the monitor began to rewind at lightning speed. Alan punched in a new command and the images

paused. Then the scene Alan had been searching for began to play.

He had come at last to the afternoon from
his childhood that had cast such a long
shadow on his life. On the screen he saw himself and Louis playing at swords with the
sticks in the half-finished building. But the
scene appeared subtly different from his
memory of it. It tcok Alan a moment to figure
out what had changed. For one, Louis's shirt
was a different color: green rather than blue.
It was strange to have such a specific memory
turn out to be wrong. Alan had seen this happen often enough with other people's lives,
but never with his own.

The timer on Hasan's screen read 105 seconds. This was very frustrating, almost unbearable. Alan felt like someone who had
been allowed to play in paradise, but only for
five minutes! Again, he had to force himself
not to linger. He needed to keep going.

"Almost . . ." Alan whispered.

Using the keyboard, he skipped ahead several minutes, hoping to arrive at just the right
moment in time. The screen still showed the
half-finished building, but now he was with

Louis on the fifth floor, high in the airy reaches of the structure. His childhood self stood halfway across the plank bridge that crossed the dangerous gap. The scene on the monitor panned upward as young Alan looked above him to the hole in the unfinished roof. The sky was clear blue with birds circling overhead, amazingly peaceful, offering no hint of the tragedy that was about to come.

Alan stared at the monitor, nervously waiting for the scene to unfold, knowing that for the first time in his life he would see it exactly as it happened rather than as he remembered it, filtered with the distortions of time. The scene panned downward from the sky. Young Alan looked over his shoulder to see Louis staring at him, standing near the edge of the gaping hole, his hand over his mouth. This was precisely as Alan remembered.

Now Alan turned from Louis and continued walking, crossing the span of the bridge. He was almost to the far side when the bridge shuddered. He looked ahead to where the plank met the edge, obviously wondering whether he could make the remaining distance. Without warning, the bridge had become unstable. Holding his breath, young Alan took a few quick steps and with a final leap, he jumped clear to the other side. Safe at last, he let out his breath and turned to face Louis, who was regarding him with boyish admiration.

Alan was thrilled to be alive. He seemed to understand at last what a foolish stunt he had pulled. Meanwhile, he had no interest in re-crossing the bridge back to where his friend was waiting. One time across was more than enough! Fortunately, there was a staircase on his side of the divide.

"Okay, I'll meet you back on the ground floor," young Alan called.

He was walking toward the stairs when Louis called to him. "Hold on!"

Alan turned to see Louis stepping up to the edge, glancing down into the abyss. Slowly, he took a cautious step onto the bridge.

"No, wait!" Alan told him.

But Louis wouldn't listen. They were boys. There was a competitive element to this game. Louis had to show that he was brave also. He took another tentative step, causing the bridge to shake. Louis put his arms out like wings for balance, but it was obvious from the start that his balance and coordination were not as good as Alan's.

"Stop!" Alan called. "Turn around. It isn't steady anymore."

But Louis kept coming, making his way slowly across the bridge, causing the plank to quiver with every step.

"Louis . . . please. Just stop," Alan pleaded.

Louis was obviously terrified, but at the same time, he was determined to prove that he could do what Alan had done. The wobbly plank had become more than a bridge. It was a rite of passage.

One step at a time, torturously, Louis continued to cross the bridge. But about two-thirds of the way across he stopped, unable to go on.

"Come on," Alan encouraged. "You're almost there."

"No," Louis told him in a frightened voice. "I can't move."

Louis tried to turn around, but he was paralyzed by his fear. The bridge rattled horribly.

"I can't move," Louis said again.

Alan stared at the bridge, watching it rattle and move. It looked very bad. At any moment, the plank could slip loose, sending

Louis crashing down five floors to his death. Louis was white as a sheet.

"Just a few more steps," Alan said, trying to keep his voice steady.

Alan stepped to the edge and reached his arms out, gesturing for Louis to come to him. Louis tried to move forward, but terror made him clumsy. All at once, his foot slipped. He tried to catch himself, but stumbled forward. In a single movement, he tripped and lunged forward, falling off the bridge. Somehow he had managed to grab hold of Alan's side of the edge, but his body dangled horribly into the hole.

The adult Alan watched this terrible moment with tears in his eyes. The timer on Hasan's computer read twenty-seven seconds. On the screen, young Alan reached forward and grabbed hold of his friend's hand. He tried to pull him up, but it was useless. Louis's hand began slipping from the other boy's grasp. Alan reached out with his other hand, frantically trying to keep Louis from falling. But he wasn't strong enough. Then came the inevitable end. And this part, sadly, was how Alan remembered.

"Wait!" Louis cried, slipping from Alan's

hold. Then suddenly Louis was tumbling down into the hole with a nightmarish cry.

Young Alan felt something tear from around Louis's neck as he dropped. Alan had closed his eyes, unable to look, so the monitor showed only blackness. When young Alan opened his eyes again, Louis's body lay five floors below amid rubble. It was a sickening moment. On the screen, the point of view went crazy as Alan's eyes darted about hysterically, as though looking for some miraculous reprieve. His breath came in gasping bursts. Finally, he opened his hand to find Louis's ivory talisman on the leather hoop resting in his palm.

Young Alan ran downstairs, careening around corners, slipping in rubble, running with all his might to get to the ground floor, where Louis lay. He came around a final corner to the wall on which he had scrawled his name earlier, yet this small fact was different from the way Alan had remembered. Instead of writing his name, he had actually drawn a doodle, a smiley face with hands. Young Alan turned from the doodle and looked at Louis's body lying motionless on the rubble. Reluctantly, he approached his new friend.

Louis was halfway on his side, motionless. But there was no blood, as in Alan's memory. Young Alan began to back away, unable to bear what his eyes were showing him. Sobbing filled his ears. And then, as Alan backed away, Louis coughed lightly—this fact registered on the Zoe, but Alan as a boy did not appear to notice, mesmerized by his own horror and guilt.

The adult Alan, hovering above the computer screen, leaned closer and turned up the volume. With the hit of a button, he rewound to the cough.

Louis was alive!

On Hasan's screen, the time read four seconds . . . three . . . two . . . one.

"Alan, unplug yourself!" Thelma cried.

"Not yet . . ."

He had to see more. On his monitor, his childhood self continued to back away, terrified and sobbing. *Clank!* What was that? Backing away, young Alan had just knocked over a can of black paint. He looked down and watched with dismay as the paint spread across the floor and all over his shoes. *But it wasn't blood, as in his memories—it was paint!*

On the screen, nine-year-old Alan turned

one final time to Louis. Louis moved his arm, very slightly. But again, young Alan had been too overcome to notice.

The adult Alan punched a button, causing the view to zoom in closer on Louis's arm. He rewound and played the scene again. Yes, Louis's arm had moved.

Alan let the scene continue. His younger self turned and began to run, then stopped when he saw the black footprints behind him. Hysterically, he began scraping his shoes against the concrete. He scraped and scraped, breathing in sharp gasps, sobbing in horror. Then, at last, without another backward glance, he ran away from the half-finished building into the street.

Meanwhile, Hasan's screen was starting to show the present danger. The green waves were peaking at crazy angles. On Alan's monitor, the Zoe images began to warp and deform. Suddenly there was a piercing beep and Alan's body jerked violently.

"Aaaaaghh!" Alan cried.

Thelma reached forward and yanked the metal disks off Alan's body. The monitor flashed white, then went dark. Alan fell backward onto a pile of equipment as Hasan leaped to his feet and rushed to his side.

"Alan!" Hasan said, grabbing and shaking him.

When Alan remained still, his pupils dilated, Hasan slapped him mightily across the face. Hassan muttered, "You stupid son of a bitch!"

Alan blinked and coughed. "I'm . . . all right."

With a huge smile, Hasan hugged him, relieved. "You don't know how close you came to having shit for brains!"

Alan managed to stand up on wobbly legs. Thelma came to his side and helped him into a seat. The monitor Alan had been using, throbbing with static, showed a dim, latent image of the construction site.

"I tried to help," Alan said in amazement, more to himself than to Thelma and Hasan. "I told him to turn around, but he didn't listen. He didn't listen."

A massive look of relief crossed Alan's face as a lifetime of guilt rose from his soul. Thelma smiled as she shut down the computers. As for Hasan, he was more than usually pleased with his amazing technical prowess. Without a doubt, this evening's work would become legendary, a story to impress young cutters many years from now.

"So you wanna take a look at the program I wrote?" Hasan asked with a grin. "If you have the time, I mean."

TWENTY

Alan was physically and mentally drained. He might have just finished a marathon. Yet his soul was at peace as he made his way home through the sleeping town. Dawn was not far away, a hint of gray in the eastern sky, the moist smell of dew in the air.

Wearily, Alan climbed the steps to his apartment. He walked down the hallway thinking only of the warm bed awaiting him. He was surprised to find the front door ajar, but too tired to care greatly. He pushed the door open to find Fletcher and Simon inside waiting for him. Simon was looking through the shelves while Fletcher stood examining the ruined Guillotine. The apartment was a mess from their searching; papers and equipment were scattered everywhere.

Fletcher spotted Alan in the doorway. Alan, of course, knew what the former cutter wanted. He had brought the ruined primary drive back with him from Hasan's apartment. With a grim smile, he took it from his coat pocket and threw it across the room. Fletcher caught it and immediately began yanking the disk from the mangled mechanism. The Zoe Implant inside had gone blue, obviously unusable.

"You'll have to find yourself another 'perfect candidate,' " Alan said.

Without any change of expression, Fletcher let the drive drop to the ground.

"Do you know how much planning it took to make Bannister's Zoe available?"

Alan shrugged. "He died of a heart complication."

Simon had stopped his searching through the shelves and came toward Alan. "*I* was the complication," Simon said in a menacing voice. "Or didn't you get to that part yet?" With a gesture of contempt, the tattooed fanatic shoved Alan against a wall.

Fletcher gazed thoughtfully at the mess

they had made. "I bet you still keep good notes," he said.

Among the papers on the floor was the red flyer that had led Alan to the synth tattoo parlor, but Fletcher hardly noticed it as he continued to search through Alan's notes. He spent nearly another twenty minutes grabbing at papers, giving them a quick once-over, then tossing them to the ground. But there was nothing to find.

"Why do you live this life?" Fletcher asked.

Alan didn't bother to answer. Fletcher would never understand. With a disgusted shake of his head, Fletcher stormed out of the apartment. Simon gave Alan a brazen stare, and for a moment Alan thought the kid was going to do something nasty just for spite. But even Simon recognized a lost cause when he saw it. In the end, he simply turned and followed in Fletcher's wake.

Alone in his apartment, Alan let out a huge sigh of relief. He felt a free man. He walked to the far end of his apartment and opened one of the windows. Sunlight flooded into his room, clean and warm and bright. Morning had come.

TWENTY-ONE

Later in the afternoon, shaved and more rested than he had felt in a very long time, Alan made a visit to the Bannister mansion. When he rang the doorbell, Rom, the Filipino butler, answered and showed him inside.

Alan stepped into the lavish hallway. Inside, the house was magnificent but it felt like a prison to Alan, a place of great unhappiness. All the money in the world could not save that family from themselves. As before, he noticed Isabel hiding behind a door that was ajar. The little girl was playing her sad spying game, eavesdropping as she had done the first time he had been there. Alan wondered if she was hoping to hear some magic word that would set her free.

Mrs. Bannister was waiting for him in the living room. Alan sat facing her on one of the huge white sofas and told her the bad news, a made-up story of how her husband's Zoe Implant had been destroyed. His own career as a cutter was finished, and though he found no particular reason to hold anything back, he left out Delila's part of the episode, not wishing to put her at the wrong end of a lawsuit. When he was finished with his tale, Mrs. Bannister sat in silence for quite a long time, absorbing the news.

"All of it?" she asked finally.

"All," he answered. "It was a terrible accident. Sometimes older Guillotine's can damage the Zoe Implants. I know there is no replacing your husband's life. He deserved a Rememory and a place in your Zoe family tree."

Jennifer Bannister gave him a shrewd look. "You will waive your fee."

"Of course."

"And you will never speak of Charles to anyone." After Alan nodded, she stood up, obviously relieved. Her voice took on a cagey tone. "What can one do? Accidents will happen. Perhaps some things are best forgotten."

Alan rose, understanding that he was being dismissed. Beyond her mother's shoulders, he saw Isabel half-hidden behind the door. He met the little girl's stare.

"Perhaps," he said.

Mrs. Bannister walked Alan to the front door. She did not appear unhappy to see him go. As for Alan, he was thrilled to leave. He was finished deleting the moments of lust and greed and violence from other people's lives.

Believing herself alone, Jennifer Bannister closed the door on the careless cutter, then turned with a start to see her daughter silently watching her. The little girl's school bag sat on the floor by the stairs.

"Oh, God, honey, you scared me!"

Isabel said nothing, but continued to stare at her mother, her face a blank.

"What's the matter?" Jennifer asked uneasily.

When the little girl didn't answer, Jennifer got down on one knee to face her. She knew she was a very fortunate woman. She was rich and beautiful, yet lines of worry played on her face.

"Isabel? What's the matter?"

The little girl backed away from her mother. "Honey . . . Isabel . . ."

But Isabel only stepped farther away. She slung her bag over her shoulder and walked back up the stairs without a word as her mother watched in torment.

When she was alone, the little girl walked through her lovely bedroom with its bright wallpaper and stuffed animals until she came to her second-story window, which looked out upon the front lawn. Isabel's Zoe Implant recorded the scene for posterity, as indeed it had recorded every scene from the beginning of her young life, every instant of what her father had done to her . . . justice perhaps waiting for some future time.

She watched Alan walk away. He had offered some strange degree of friendship—a friendship she did not entirely understand, though it filled her with hope.

As she watched, Alan headed across the grounds, slipped out the gate, and disappeared around the corner.

TWENTY-TWO

The late-afternoon sun came down in a slant of dusty golden light on the street outside of Delila's bookstore, filling Alan with a sense of beauty and loss. He didn't want to lose Delila, but he knew very well how badly he had behaved with her. Many things were clear to him now that earlier had been obscured. Too late, he feared.

He stood on the sidewalk for a long time, watching her through the glass of the store window, getting up the nerve to go inside. There were no customers at that time of afternoon, yet still he hesitated. At last he walked through the door, setting the tinkly little bell in motion.

Delila looked up from where she was

seated reading a book and saw him. "You must be joking." Her voice was flat and uninviting.

Alan had rehearsed his first lines. "I can't ask for forgiveness. I just want to be heard."

She shook her head. "I've had it with your lies, Hakman."

Alan took a breath and continued with what he had planned to say, rushing ahead. "As a cutter, I see the worst in people," he explained. "How could I love another person when I know what people are really like? But one day . . . I saw you . . . and you were different than the others."

She stood and wandered back through the aisles of the store, searching absently for a book. "You fell in love with an image of me, not with me."

"At first," he admitted, following her through the store. "But now it's the real you I want. The way you really are."

"How can I believe you after what you did to me?"

"That's all over. I've quit. I'll never cut again. No more lies, no more secrets." When she paused, Alan took her hand and guided it to the back of his neck. "Look."

Her fingers felt the outline of his synth tattoo. "What's that?"

"It's proof to you that this time things will be different. The tattoo . . . I got it for you. It means I have a Zoe Implant. No cutter can have a Zoe Implant. And so you see, there's no turning back."

Delila glanced away, obviously conflicted. Alan felt his entire life hanging in the balance. At least she hadn't thrown him out of the bookstore yet. As long as she was willing to listen and talk, he had a chance.

"You watched his life, Alan . . . and mine," she added after a moment.

This was a complicated matter. Even Delila had her secrets, her guilt, the mistakes she had made over the course of her lifetime that she didn't wish others to know. The desire for privacy was only natural, after all. But a cutter saw everything.

"There are parts you didn't see. He had forgiven you," Alan told her quietly. "You were the only beautiful thing in his life."

Delila lowered her eyes and didn't respond. Alan saw it was useless, at least for the present. He was turning to go when, to his surprise, she stopped him.

"Okay, Alan," she said. "I don't understand it all, but I'm willing to try one more time. But I have my own test for you."

That evening, Delila came to his apartment. Alan had everything cleaned up. All the shelves had been cleared and emptied into boxes on the floor. He had also taken down the many mirrors, stacking them in a corner with their faces to the wall. His professional life had been tidied up as well. The Guillotine was shut down forever, with the Chop Block closed on top. The framed Cutters' Code, which had once guided his life, lay faceup inside one of the boxes.

Alan sat on the couch near the window. Delila stood with her back to him. He had no idea what she had in mind. She turned with a sly look on her face and took off the scarf that was around her neck, holding it toward him in both hands.

"What's this for?" he asked.

Without a word, she slowly tied the scarf around his eyes and then led him to the bed. For Alan the experience was strange, yet delightful. Playfully, he held his hands out in front of him, imitating a blind man. Delila took one of his hands and guided it to her face.

How smooth her skin was! He touched her cheekbones, her nose, her brow. He felt like a child walking for the first time. Slowly, Alan's fingers traced the contours of Delila's face, moving downward to her neck and shoulders. The touching was surprisingly erotic. After a while, Delila took his other hand and placed it on her thigh. He let his hand move up her leg, tickling her lightly.

She laughed. "Not like that!"

Alan smiled, feeling happier than he had for a very long time. He let his hands move over her soft curves and warm feminine places. The sensation was absolute magic. It was wonderful to be blindfolded, to touch her so simply . . . and, no, he didn't need to watch!

Suddenly, life seemed perfectly easy. With no effort at all, they fell back together on the bed. In the darkness, Alan felt himself joined with her, first in passion and then in utter peace.

TWENTY-THREE

The cemetery at the edge of the city was enormous, with rolling green lawns that seemingly went on forever, undulating across the land, dotted with hundreds of white gravestones. It was a city of the dead: those who were forgotten and those whose memories lived on forever, thanks to Eye Tech.

On a quiet afternoon, Alan wandered across the well-tended paths looking for the grave of Louis Hunt, his old friend and nemesis. He felt the peacefulness of the day and was in no hurry. He passed a woman sitting on the grass in front of a gravestone that had a video screen embedded in the marble. Alan stopped to watch as the woman plugged a set of earphones into an outlet on the side of the gravestone, then sat watching and listening as the Zoe film of the dead person began to play. Soon the woman was sobbing with emotion, reliving the life that was gone.

Alan turned away, moving on with a bitter-sweet feeling, searching among the rows of the dead for Louis Hunt. About half of the headstones had Zoe screens installed. He was no longer certain whether the Zoe technology was good or bad. Perhaps it was best for each person to decide. Certainly, it was beyond his own scope to figure out.

Wandering up and down the maze of paths, Alan finally found the headstone he was seeking. There was no Zoe screen, only a simple epitaph engraved on the stone:

LOUIS HUNT
GONE TOO SOON,
ALWAYS IN OUR MEMORIES

Alan stood quietly in front of the grave for a long time, deep in thought. A single after-noon had joined Louis and him together for-ever, an odd intersection of memory and fate. Alan had carried the guilt of his childhood mistake as an incredible burden that had crip-

pled his life. It was a terrible thing to believe
he had caused the death of another human
being. But for Alan, the guilt was finished,
and he felt only simple affection for this un-
likely kid with thick glasses who had made
him suffer, but had taught him so much.
Memories were fine, but in the end, it was
best perhaps simply to release them. Rather
than hang on, he'd let them go free, like the
dried leaves of autumn tossed on the
wind. . . .

He understood exactly what it was that was
so wrong about Zoe Implants. Perhaps after
all it was best to let human memory fade
away, to join the elements, to cease. Or at
least, that conclusion is what Alan came to as
he stood in silence by Louis Hunt's grave.
After a long time, he reached beneath his collar and removed the ivory talisman from
around his neck, his memento from that long-
ago afternoon. Kneeling, he placed the talisman on the grave. With that act, he and Louis
were finished. It was time for Alan to get on
with his life. He was rising to his feet when
he heard footsteps coming up behind him.

"A friend?"

He turned and was surprised to see

Fletcher. He wasn't certain what more they had to discuss. "Something like that," Alan replied vaguely.

"I hear you're not cutting anymore."

Alan nodded, hoping to put an end to the conversation. "I think I've had enough of other people's lives."

Alan turned to walk away. But unfortunately, Fletcher wasn't finished.

"Stop, Alan. I can't let you go."

Alan turned back to face his old colleague, confused as to what the other man could possibly want. Weren't their drama and conflict finished? Then he saw that Fletcher was holding one of the red anti-Zoe Implant flyers in his fist.

"Word travels fast in my circles," Fletcher said. "Word is, a cutter came in for a synth tattoo. Word is that cutter was you."

Fletcher stared hard at Alan and spotted the synth tattoo, with its unmistakable pattern and colors. Like magic, a gun had appeared in Fletcher's hand. Alan hadn't see him reach for it, but the barrel was pointed at his chest.

"What's this?" Alan asked, still not getting it.

"Don't move," Fletcher told him.

"You saw Bannister's Implant. It's junked," Alan told him. "I have nothing you want."

Fletcher shook his head. "Bannister's footage is gone, but you've seen his life. And it's encrypted into *your* Zoe."

For Alan, the world seemed to slow down as he realized the awful truth. Charles Bannister's life was enclosed within his own visual memories. He simply hadn't been thinking about Zoe Implants, his own or others. His life had moved on to other things.

With a click, Fletcher cocked his revolver. The sound snapped Alan out of his paralysis. Fletcher was going to kill him! It didn't seem fair, not when he had everything to live for. Delila was waiting for him back at her little bookstore. But Fletcher, of course, cared about none of Alan's concerns. The fanatical resolve was plain in his eyes.

Suddenly, Alan was angry. He'd had it with Fletcher and his group of crazies. Pro-Zoe, anti-Zoe, it was all the same to Alan. He refused to stand there and be a victim. Without a word, Alan turned abruptly and dashed off across the graves.

"No!" Fletcher shouted, taking off after him.

Alan headed off across the rolling lawns of the cemetery, running as fast as he could. He dived past gravestones and startled mourners. A shot rang out behind him. The bullet shattered a tombstone nearby, sending up a cloud of dust and shattered stone. Alan kept running, breathing hard, zigzagging among the graves to make himself a more difficult target.

He made his way running across the open hill until he reached a fenced-off area of elaborate tombs for the wealthy. The miniature neoclassic temples, many of them of dubious taste, were complete with winged angels standing guard. Several of the tombs had huge screens on one side for Rememory films. Alan saw only a possible place to hide. He sped through the maze of gaudy temples, up and down the rows of the dead hoping to lose Fletcher. Running crazily, he came around a corner and ducked behind one of the larger tombs, a hideous thing of dark marble built to resemble a miniature Acropolis.

For the moment, Fletcher was nowhere in sight. Had Alan lost him? He wasn't sure. Alan bent over, trying to catch his breath. His lungs ached. For the moment, he appeared to be safe, but it was unsettling not to know where Fletcher was. When Alan's breathing eased, he peered cautiously around the far end of the tomb. There was still no sign of Fletcher. Alan could see nothing but a row of tombs, silent and cold.

Alan slid back along the wall of the tomb to the other corner. Carefully, he peeked around the edge. Fletcher, with his gun ready, was standing calmly only a dozen feet away, near a black marble tomb.

Fletcher fired. The sickening explosion echoed through the necropolis. The bullet missed Alan but hit the Zoe screen of a nearby tomb behind him. Without warning, a Rememory began to play with garbled audio. Static electricity spat out from the bullet hole as significant moments of the dead person's life sped through at a crazy speed: baptism, high school graduation ceremony, wedding, and more. Fletcher paused to stare at the bizarre sight.

Alan took advantage of the distraction to dash between two tombs. He ran as fast as he could through the graves with Fletcher close behind. Alan came to a small hill and picked up speed, running down toward a fence at the end of the cemetery. With a little luck, he could climb over the fence and get away.

But then he tripped on either a rock or a tuft of grass. Suddenly he was rolling and gagging on a mouthful of grass. When he managed to look up, Fletcher was only a few feet away, raising his gun and taking aim.

There was nothing more Alan could do. He looked up helplessly into Fletcher's eyes, awaiting death. Everything seemed to move in slow motion as the gun barrel rose.

But the seconds continued and Alan found himself still alive. It was incredible, but Fletcher was struggling with himself, unable to pull the trigger. He couldn't shoot! Slowly, Fletcher lowered the gun to his side.

Alan rose unsteadily to his feet. He hesitated briefly, giving Fletcher a quick, curious look. But he didn't wait for a second chance. With calm deliberation, he turned and walked away.

He was free, filled with thoughts of Delila and the new life that awaited him, when the gunshot rang out, fading slowly into the quiet of the afternoon.

TWENTY-FOUR

Delila was in her store organizing books on a shelf when she had an odd feeling that she was being watched. She wasn't expecting Alan, but she never knew when he might pop by the store. He liked to surprise her, coming by with some present or just to say hello, especially now when things were going so well between them. She glanced up toward the window to where he often stood watching her. But the sidewalk outside was empty. Alan wasn't there.

Puzzled, Delila continued to stare at the window, searching, until she realized she must have been mistaken. At last, with an uncomfortable sense of emptiness, she returned to her work.

*   *   *

In the cemetery, the gunshot continued to reverberate, an endless ringing in the sky. Fletcher looked about wildly, trying to see where the shot had come from. He had not fired. His revolver remained motionless at his side.

Alan stumbled backward. He did an awkward little dance, then collapsed on the ground, shot in the back. It was only then that Fletcher saw Simon outside the fence, standing calmly with a gun smoking in his hand. The shot had come from Simon's gun.

Fletcher felt a surge of anger mixed with hopelessness and despair. He rushed over to where Alan lay dying on the grass. He was sprawled on his stomach in an awkward position. Very carefully, Fletcher turned Alan over, trying to be as gentle as possible. Blood soaked through Alan's shirt.

Alan was still alive, but barely. He gazed upward and gradually his eyes focused, seeing Fletcher above him, the face of his enemy blocking out the sky. Alan wished Fletcher would move aside because the sky behind him was beautiful. But Fletcher wasn't going anywhere. He was studying Alan with concern: his eyes haunted, his lips slightly open as though he were about to cry out some saving word. It took Alan a moment to recognize the expression on Fletcher's face. It was guilt. Guilt to torment and pull at your soul. Guilt to know that you were responsible for another person's death. It was the same kind of guilt Alan had experienced all too well himself. Fletcher's mouth seemed to form the words, "I'm sorry."

Meanwhile, Simon had vaulted the fence. Fletcher gave the young man a quick look of utter contempt, then returned his attention to Alan.

"There was no other way," Fletcher said finally. His voice was full of anguish, the sound of a man trying to convince himself.

Alan no longer cared. He felt no pain, only an encroaching numbness that seemed to overcome his body. He stared up at Fletcher as his life drained away. Fletcher had just noticed that his hands were covered with Alan's blood. With a frantic gesture, Fletcher tried to wipe the blood off his hands on the grass. Alan smiled. The scene reminded him of something so long ago and far away, he couldn't recall precisely what it was.

With a great effort, Alan raised his hands in front of his face. They, too, were drenched in his blood, but somehow it was all right. Blood and sunlight and sky. All his guilt, washed away . . .

The Zoe Implant recorded everything, without sound because of the synth tattoo.

Alan lowered his hands, and there were the cemetery, endless and beautiful, and the sky, clear and blue, darkening into twilight, and birds circling high overhead.

And then . . . slowly . . . came darkness.

TWENTY-FIVE

A rewind symbol appeared in the upper corner of the screen. Alan Hakman's life began to play backward at lightning speed, beginning with his death at the cemetery, returning through the long years.

Fletcher sat at his Guillotine in his dusty basement cutting room with a dozen monitors going, each alive with a different moment of Alan's life. One screen showed Alan's birth: a bright light at the end of a long tunnel. Another screen showed Alan talking to Isabel Bannister in her bedroom, while a third had Alan at his Guillotine, looking into monitors where scenes of Charles Bannister's life played. Many of the monitors showed documents and Eye Tech contracts scrolling by.

There were other Zoe projects as well flashing by on the monitors, Danny Monroe's life, even the experimental dog Zoe, everything that Alan had ever seen. One monitor showed Alan staring into a mirror, studying himself with haunted, unhappy eyes. And another showed Alan sitting at a Guillotine with a younger Thelma and a very young Fletcher seated beside her.

Fletcher suddenly felt a deep sense of loss and nostalgia. What he was doing brought him no joy. His eyes were sad and regretful. Alan was free, but he was not.

"It's for the greater good, Alan," Fletcher whispered to the many images running past him. "Your life will mean something. I promise you."

Around his neck, Fletcher wore the ivory talisman passed down from Louis Hunt to Alan and now to him. In every sense, Fletcher was the inheritor of Alan's life: his memories, his hopes, and his crushing guilt.

Fletcher's eyes turned to a monitor on which young Alan was walking with Louis near the construction site. The two boys were counting their marbles, unaware of the disaster that awaited them. The name and age display in the lower right-hand corner read:

A. HAKMAN: 9 YEARS: 43 DAYS:
12 HOURS

"What's your name?" nine-year-old Alan asked his new friend.

"Louis. Yours?"

"Alan," he replied.

Just then, Alan's Zoe Implant caught the moment perfectly. The view from his childhood eyes panning forever upward to the unfinished building, empty and abandoned, and the burning sky beyond.